D

1

P

h

K

th

E

h

s

H

E

th

S

Causing Chaos
with
Jeremy James

David Henry Wilson

Illustrated by Axel Scheffler

MACMILLAN CHILDREN'S BOOKS

Can a Spider Learn to Fly? first published 1984 under the title *How to Stop a Train with One Finger* by J. M. Dent & Sons Ltd
Do Goldfish Play the Violin? first published 1985 by J. M. Dent & Sons Ltd
Please Keep Off the Dinosaur first published 1993 by Pan Macmillan Children's Books

This edition published 2006 by Macmillan Children's Books
a division of Macmillan Publishers Limited
20 New Wharf Road, London N1 9RR
Basingstoke and Oxford
Associated companies throughout the world
www.panmacmillan.com

ISBN 978-0-330-44175-9

3 5 7 9 8 6 4

A CIP catalogue record for this book is available from
the British Library.

Typeset by Intype Libra Ltd
Printed and bound in the UK by CPI Mackays, Chatham ME5 8TD

Can a Spider Learn to Fly?

For Herta Ryda

Contents

CHAPTER ONE

Red Between the Lines

Jeremy James and Daddy were going on a train journey. It should have been a car journey, but Daddy's car had had one of its coughing and shuddering attacks and was now recovering in the repair shop. Daddy had an appointment in Castlebury, which was fifty miles away, and so while Mummy stayed at home to look after Christopher and Jennifer (she said twin babies weren't much fun on public transport, but Jeremy James thought twin babies weren't much fun anywhere), Daddy and Jeremy James set out to catch the 10.15 train.

By the time Daddy had found his wallet, papers, briefcase and left sock, it was nearly ten o'clock, and Daddy said they would have to run to catch the train. Jeremy James didn't think he could run fast enough to catch any train, but he held on to Daddy's hand, and the two of them ran-walked and walked-ran all the way to the station.

'Three minutes to go,' said Daddy, puffing like an old steam engine. 'Let's hope the train'll be late.'

They bought the tickets and went panting (Daddy)

and scampering (Jeremy James) up a steep slope and on to a long grey platform. This contained a few people and a lot of litter.

'Exactly 10.15!' gasped Daddy. 'Train must be late. Lucky for us.'

At that moment a crackly voice boomed from up in the roof: 'We regret to announce that the 10.15 train to worple, worple, Castlebury, worple, worple and worple is running approximately forty minutes late.'

'Forty minutes!' exclaimed Daddy. 'Ugh, what a service!'

'I thought we *wanted* the train to be late,' said Jeremy James.

'Well yes,' said Daddy, 'but not *that* late!'

2

Just then there was a distant rattle that grew into a rumble that suddenly became a terrifying roar, and a train hurtled through on the other side of the track. The station and Jeremy James shook like a couple of jellies in a thunderstorm. Then the roar faded to a rumble, a rattle, and finally silence, and the station and Jeremy James stopped shivering.

Jeremy James gazed up the track with a worried expression on his face.

'What's the matter, Jeremy James?' asked Daddy.

'Well,' said Jeremy James, 'if the train's going *that* fast, I don't think I shall be able to get on it.'

Daddy laughed. 'If the train's going,' he said, 'you shouldn't *try* to get on it. You only get on trains that stop.'

At 10.55 the 10.15 train to Castlebury stopped for Daddy and Jeremy James. It came slithering painfully into the station like a giant snake with backache, and Daddy helped Jeremy James up the high steps and into the carriage. Most of the seats were empty.

'There aren't many people,' said Jeremy James.

'They've probably gone on ahead,' said Daddy. 'On foot.'

Jeremy James sat down by a window, and Daddy sat opposite him. There was a whistle, and the train twitched, jerked, and began to slide gently out of the station.

'We're moving,' said Jeremy James.

'Let us be thankful,' said Daddy, 'for small miracles.'

In the wide frame of the window, houses and factories and back gardens gave way to fields and trees and rivers. The train diddly-dummed along, and Jeremy James leaned back and looked round. There was nothing very interesting to see – seats, tables, Daddy, the luggage rack, Daddy's briefcase on the luggage rack . . . and above Daddy's briefcase a red handle.

'Daddy, what's the red handle for?' asked Jeremy James.

Daddy followed the direction of Jeremy James's pointing finger.

'Ah, the communication cord,' said Daddy. 'It's so that people can stop the train in an emergency.'

'You mean like wanting to wee?' asked Jeremy James.

That had happened to him once. They'd been driving along the motorway and he'd had an emergency, so Daddy had stopped at the side of the road. Then a police car had come along, and the policeman and Daddy had had a lovely conversation about emergencies.

'No,' said Daddy. 'If it's *that* sort of emergency, there's a lavatory at the end of the carriage.'

A little while later, Daddy himself had *that* sort of emergency, and he went off, leaving Jeremy James to look out of the window. The train was going quite slowly now, past big gloomy buildings and a lot of railway lines. Perhaps they were coming into a station – one of the worples before Castlebury. Jeremy James hoped Daddy would get back before the train stopped, in case someone wanted to take his seat. But if the worst came to the worst, he could tell them that Daddy was doing an emergency.

It was indeed a station. Jeremy James stood up to get a better view. There were quite a lot of people on the platform, and Jeremy James spotted a crowd of children. The train glided by, and he waved to them. Some of them waved back, and he wished the train would stop just there, but on it went . . . and on . . . and on. And all of a sudden, they were out of the station again! They hadn't stopped at all!

Obviously something had gone wrong. Those people were waiting for the train, but of course they weren't allowed to get on it unless it stopped, and it hadn't stopped. Perhaps the children hadn't been waving to him but to the driver, trying to attract his attention. Perhaps the driver had been looking the wrong way. Or perhaps he was asleep. Or dead. Dead, and slumped over the steering wheel, while the train roared on and on towards disaster and destruction.

There was no doubt about it, this was an emergency. Jeremy James leapt on to the seat, clutched the luggage rack with one hand, put one foot on Daddy's armrest, heaved himself up, and was just able to reach the red handle and give it a hearty tug.

Almost at once there was a grinding screech, and it felt as if the train were trying to move backwards while everything inside it tried to move forwards.

Jeremy James bounced from armrest to seat to floor, and lay there for a moment wondering how much of himself he'd left hanging on the luggage rack. Then he picked himself up, and checked that all of him was still where it was supposed to be. He found that even his nose was still sitting comfortably in the middle of his face, and soon he was pressing it against the window to see if the children and the other passengers were coming.

Wouldn't everybody be pleased! Jeremy James had saved the outside passengers from missing their train, and the inside from disaster. When they found out what had happened, the railway people would probably give him a very big reward.

But the children and other passengers didn't come. Daddy came, closely followed by a railway person who had not brought along a big reward. All he brought with him was a peaked cap, a bristly moustache, and a very red face. He didn't seem pleased at all. In fact he was very un-pleased. He said someone had pulled the red handle, and he wanted to know *who* had pulled the red handle, and *why* the red handle had been pulled. Jeremy James explained to him that some people were waiting for this train at the station, and the driver hadn't seen them because he was dead, and so he, Jeremy James, had pulled the red handle in order to save everybody, and would there be a reward?

The red-faced man's face went redder, and Daddy's face went as red as the red-faced man's had

been before it went redder. The people at the station, said the redder-faced man, were not waiting for *this* train, and the driver wasn't dead, and there were two passengers on this train who might end up dead after the driver had heard why the red handle had been pulled, and there would not be a reward, and grown men should learn to control their children, and there'd already been enough trouble today without . . .

The red-faced man now used a word that Daddy had once used when hammering a nail (his thumbnail) into the wall. Mummy had said that such words were forbidden, but the red-faced man obviously didn't know Mummy had forbidden such words, and after he'd said it twice Daddy went back up the aisle with him.

Jeremy James sat in the corner and looked up at the red handle near Daddy's briefcase. It reminded him of when he'd been on a bus with Mummy. Instead of a handle there'd been a bell, and when the conductor wanted the bus to stop or start he rang the bell. The thought occurred to Jeremy James that if he pulled the handle again, the train might start and the red-faced man would go away.

Jeremy James was just climbing on to Daddy's seat when Daddy came back along the aisle, looking a little sadly at his wallet.

'*Now* what are you up to?' asked Daddy.

Jeremy James explained his idea to Daddy. But Daddy didn't think it was a very good idea.

'Your ideas, Jeremy James,' said Daddy, 'have made a late train later, a red face redder, and poor Daddy a lot poorer. So I think the best idea, Jeremy James, is for you to stop having ideas altogether.'

The train was now moving again, and so Jeremy James sat quietly in the corner and looked out of the window. It wasn't easy to stop having ideas – in fact ideas kept coming to him all the time. He had ideas about ice cream, and chicken, and sweets, and fizzy drinks. He also had an idea about saying he was sorry he'd pulled the red handle. But he didn't tell Daddy and so Daddy never knew.

CHAPTER TWO

To Be Or Not To Be

Daddy and Jeremy James had lunch in Castlebury. Daddy said he fancied some Chinese food, and Jeremy James said he fancied *any* food, so they went to a Chinese restaurant. Daddy ordered something strange-sounding and strange-looking, and Jeremy James ordered chicken and chips. Chinese chicken and chips looked and tasted just like English chicken and chips, and so did Chinese ice cream and Chinese Coca-Cola.

When lunch was over ('I like Chinese food,' said Jeremy James), they walked through the streets, stopping only to look in a bookshop and nearly to look in a toyshop, until they came to a large building with pillars, posters, photographs, and a crowd of people in the entrance.

Daddy told Jeremy James that this was the theatre, and the people were waiting to see a play. Jeremy James wondered if they would like to see *him* play, but Daddy didn't think they would. 'Besides,' said Daddy, 'we've got to go and meet a very important man.'

They went past the crowd of people, up a stair-case, and into a corridor at the end of which was an open door. Daddy knocked, and poked his head round it.

'Hello, John!' said a cheerful voice from inside.

'Hello, Malcolm,' said Daddy, and he and Jeremy James entered the room. It was a very untidy room with papers, posters, pictures and books everywhere. If Mummy had seen this room, she would have told Malcolm to tidy it immediately.

'This is Jeremy James,' said Daddy. 'Jeremy James, this is Malcolm Crawford who runs the theatre.'

'Hello, Jeremy James,' said Malcolm, who had a sort of upside-down face, with a lot of hair on his chin and none on his head.

'Are you important?' asked Jeremy James.

'Well, I am to me,' said Malcolm. 'Are you import-ant to you?'

'Yes,' said Jeremy James.

'Then we're both important,' said Malcolm. 'Sally!'

A fair-haired girl came in from the office next door, and smiled at Jeremy James.

'Now would you two like something to drink?' asked Malcolm.

'No, thanks,' said Daddy. 'We've just had lunch.'

'Yes, please,' said Jeremy James.

It was decided that Jeremy James should go next door with Sally, have his drink, and perhaps do some drawing while Daddy and Malcolm talked about the things they had to talk about. And so off went Jeremy James with Sally, who duly supplied him with his second Coca-Cola, and his first paper and pencil of the day. When Jeremy James had finished eating, drinking, and burping, he sat at a table drawing a train, while Sally sat at her desk and typed letters at ten times the speed of raindrops.

If Sally had continued typing, Jeremy James might well have continued drawing, and the afternoon would have passed quite undramatically. But Sally had to go and see somebody.

'I shan't be long,' she said. 'You'll be all right on your own for a little while, won't you?'

Jeremy James said he would, and he was. For a little while. But the little while grew into a bigger while, and the train was finished, the station was finished, and the red-faced man with a moustache was finished. And drawing was boring anyway. From the office next door he could hear Daddy and Malcolm worpling on, and the thought occurred to him that if people were playing in the theatre, they might let him play with them – at least until Daddy and Malcolm had finished worpling.

Jeremy James opened the door of Sally's office and stepped out into the corridor. It was empty. And so was the staircase, and the next corridor, and the room he peeped into . . . wasn't that a noise from behind the door at the end of the passage? Music, and then voices. Could the people be playing there?

Jeremy James slipped through the door, and found

himself in darkness. But there was light further along, and the voices were very clear now – an old man was telling someone to read a book. That didn't sound much fun, but perhaps Jeremy James could persuade them to play something else. Another man was talking now – not quite so old as the first, but not young either. It wasn't going to be easy to play if everyone was old, only whoever was supposed to be reading was sure to be young. Grown-ups are always telling children to read or draw or do something boring.

Jeremy James could see a little more clearly now that his eyes had grown used to the darkness. He was standing behind what looked like walls with gaps between them. The lights and voices were coming from the other side of these walls, and so all he had to do was walk through one of the gaps.

'I hear him coming; let's withdraw, my lord,' said the old man's voice.

That was a surprise. Jeremy James had not realized that anyone knew he was there, but perhaps they were going to play hide-and-seek with him. Quickly he walked through the gap and into the light, hoping to see the old man before he hid. The light was so strong, though, that at first he could see nothing. From beyond the light, which was shining on him from all angles, came a loud murmur, followed by a sort of tittering noise. Then, through a gap in the wall opposite, there came a young man with fair hair, a wispy beard, and the strangest black clothes that Jeremy James had ever seen.

'To be, or not to be,' said the young man. 'That is the question.'

'Hello,' said Jeremy James.

A look of surprise came on to the young man's face, and there was some loud laughter from beyond the bright lights.

'Get off!' said the young man quietly, without opening his lips.

'Off what?' asked Jeremy James.

'Get off the stage!' hissed the young man.

Jeremy James looked down, but as he didn't seem to be standing on anything in particular, he stayed where he was.

'Why are you wearing those funny clothes?' he asked.

There was now a great roar of laughter from beyond the lights, and Jeremy James screwed up his eyes to try and see who was there. He could just make out some rows of faces, and they all seemed to be looking in his direction, as if he was a sort of television set.

Jeremy James turned to the young man, who was looking wildly around like someone who's lost a bar of chocolate.

'What are we playing?' asked Jeremy James.

The young man called out: 'Curtain!' which was a game Jeremy James had never heard of, but just at that same moment an old man came in, wearing a long brown robe and a long white beard.

'Ah, 'tis the First Player's son!' said the old man.

14

'No, I'm not,' said Jeremy James. 'I'm Daddy's son.'

'Come along, my lad,' said the old man, bustling towards Jeremy James. Then to the young man he added: 'My Lord, I'll see that he is safely stowed.'

He put his hand on Jeremy James's arm, and Jeremy James found himself looking up into a face that wasn't a real face at all. It was old, but the lines were not wrinkles – they were drawings in black. And the eyebrows, which had seemed bushy and white from a distance, were not bushy and white in reality – they were fluffed up and painted. And as for the long white beard – Jeremy James had seen a long white beard like that before. It had been at Christmas, and Jeremy James had gone to a party where the Reverend Cole had pretended he was Santa Claus. He'd worn a beard just like this one, and it had fallen off when Jeremy James had shown everyone that this Santa Claus was not the real Santa Claus.

'Are you pretending to be Santa Claus?' Jeremy James asked the old man holding his arm.

The laughter from beyond the lights was now almost as loud as the train that had roared through the station.

'Come along, you little horror!' muttered the old man, and pulled Jeremy James towards a gap in the wall.

Jeremy James didn't like being pulled along by a fake Santa Claus, and somehow in the struggle the old man got his legs caught in his robe and went tumbling head first down to the ground. This was greeted by a thunderclap of cheering and applause which continued as he clambered to his feet, tucked Jeremy James under one arm, and hurried off through the gap and into the darkness.

Waiting in the darkness were some other shadowy figures that Jeremy James couldn't see properly now that his eyes were used to the bright light.

'Who is he?' whispered one.

'How did he get in?'

'He should be skinned alive!'

'We've got to get rid of him.'

Jeremy James began to find these dark figures and angry mutterings rather frightening, but then he heard a woman's voice that was a little less frightening:

'I'll take him. Give him to me.'

A hand grasped him, and he was led away through the darkness, out of a door, and into a lighted corridor. The lady holding his hand was Sally.

'Oh dear,' said Sally, 'you *are* going to get us into trouble.'

'Why?' asked Jeremy James.

'Because you weren't supposed to go in there,' said Sally. 'And I shouldn't have left you on your own. I'll tell you what. Shall we keep it a secret, just between ourselves?'

'You mean like the price of Mummy's new dress?' asked Jeremy James.

'That's right,' said Sally. 'We'll just pretend you've been in my office all afternoon.'

And so Jeremy James and Sally headed for the office, stopping only to buy a large bar of chocolate at the refreshment counter on the way. Then Sally sat typing, and Jeremy James sat drawing and eating, while Daddy and Malcolm worpled in the office next door.

When Daddy at last poked his head in, Jeremy James had done three drawings and eaten twelve squares of chocolate, and Sally had done twelve letters and eaten three squares of chocolate.

'Time to go, Jeremy James,' said Daddy. 'Sally, how did you manage to keep him so quiet?'

'Oh, I just left him to entertain himself,' said Sally.

Jeremy James said goodbye to Sally, who gave him a kiss, and to Malcolm, who shook his hand, and then he and Daddy went down the staircase and out into the entrance hall of the theatre. From behind a closed door, Jeremy James could just hear the voice of a woman singing:

> *'And will he not come again?*
> *And will he not come again?'*

'I wonder if she means me,' said Jeremy James.

'And why should she mean you?' asked Daddy.

Jeremy James gave a little smile and took Daddy's hand as they went out of the theatre.

'*That*,' he said, looking back while his legs walked forward, 'is the question.'

CHAPTER THREE

Eight Hairy Legs

There was a spider in the bath. Jeremy James was sitting on the lavatory, and he just happened to look sideways and downwards, and there was the spider. It wasn't one of those tiny, tickly ones – he didn't mind those. No, it was one of those large leg-spreading ones, black and hairy and shuddery – the sort that make your backbone run up and down your body.

It's not easy to think about other things when there's a black spider sprawling less than three feet away from your bare legs. At any moment it could come scrabbling up the bath and on to your foot, legs, tummy . . . ugh! Besides, where there's one spider there could be other spiders, and there's just no telling where they might crawl to. Jeremy James immediately felt a goose-pimply tingle at the back of his neck, and slapped it hard to make sure the goose-pimple didn't creep down on to his back. Then the thought occurred to him that if a spider got into the bath, another spider might get into the lavatory, and then just think where that could creep to! He leapt off the seat and looked into the pan. Nothing.

He looked down into the bath again, just in time to see the spider take a quick scuttly step towards the plughole. Then it stopped still again, legs slightly bent, as if tensed to do a mighty leap. If it leapt out of the bath, Jeremy James decided he would leap out of the bathroom. But what should he do if it stayed in the bath?

Jeremy James remembered a spider that had once been hanging on his bedroom wall. He had known then that he'd never be able to sleep while it was there, and so he'd taken his bedroom slipper and given the spider a whack. But the result had been a horrible mess. Half the spider had been squelched into the wall, and the other half had been squelched into the slipper, and Mummy had had to come and wipe all the bits and pieces away with a wet cloth. Even then, Jeremy James hadn't slept very well, because he kept imagining spider-legs running all over him.

On another occasion he'd called for Daddy, and Daddy had arrived with a large sheet of newspaper.

'Let's have a look then,' Daddy had said, and with the newspaper spread wide he had advanced on the spider and had suddenly jammed the paper against the wall and at great speed screwed it up into a big ball.

'He won't trouble you any more,' Daddy had said. 'He's either dead or studying the sports news.'

But Jeremy James had seen something Daddy had not seen, and he asked Daddy to unscrew the paper again. And when Daddy unscrewed the paper, he found to his surprise that there was nothing there except the sports news. Then they had spent half an hour trying in vain to attract a spider that clearly wasn't interested in sport. That had been another sleepless night.

Well, at least this was morning, and the spider was in the bathroom, not the bedroom. But the problem was the same – how do you get rid of a spider without making it into a mess or a magic vanishing act?

The spider twitched and twiddled itself one step nearer the plughole. Jeremy James had an idea. Another few steps and it would be near enough for him to turn the tap on and swoosh it away down the hole. No mess at all. In fact, as clean an end as you could wish for.

'Move!' said Jeremy James. 'Go on! Shoo! Quick march!'

The spider did not even slow-march. Jeremy James stood and looked at the spider, and the spider stood and looked at Jeremy James. This was not going to be easy. Jeremy James needed a weapon, and his eye fell on the bathbrush. A scratch with those bristles should make even the toughest spider jump. It might even take the brush for a monster with a moustache and die of fright.

Jeremy James ran the bathbrush along the bottom of the bath, until the bristles were almost touching what might be the spider's eighth little toenail. The spider remained very still. Jeremy James moved the brush again so that it just touched the tip of the

21

spidery toe. The spider twitched. Probably thought it had an itch. Jeremy James pushed the brush firmly against the spider's leg. With a scurry and a flurry the spider raced forward, while Jeremy James leapt back and dropped the brush in the bath with a clatter.

Now his heart was jumping like a grasshopper with hiccups. This was turning out to be a dangerous battle. In the past he'd killed snakes and crocodiles and man-eating tigers in the bath, but none of them had given him half as much trouble as this spider. There it lurked, hairy legs spread wide apart, waiting to pounce and cover him with shivers. Two inches away from the plughole.

Gradually Jeremy James's heart sat down again in his chest. If he could just push the spider with the brush and then whoosh it with the tap, he could send it sailing down the Seven Seas. On the other hand, it might grab hold of the brush and come racing over the bristles, handle, hand, arm . . .

Heroes don't think about 'might-be's. Jeremy James leaned over the bath, picked up the brush, and with eyes swivelling like tennis-watchers he reached for the tap nearest the spider.

Swoosh and sweep! Down came the water and the brush, and as the spider struggled to swim up the bath, so Jeremy James pushed it down again. But the flow of water kept bringing the spider back up the bath. Jeremy James turned the tap off, and the water sucked the spider back towards the hole.

'Down you go!' said Jeremy James.

And with eight despairing waves and a loud gurgle, the spider disappeared from view.

Bathbrush in hand, Jeremy James stood triumphant.

'Jeremy James!' came Mummy's voice from the landing. 'Haven't you finished in there?'

'I've just been killing a spider,' said Jeremy James.

'Well hurry up. I'm waiting to bath the twins!' called Mummy.

'It was a huge spider!' said Jeremy James. 'And it nearly killed *me*!'

But Mummy didn't seem interested. Perhaps she might have been more interested if the spider *had* killed Jeremy James. Then she might have wished she'd thought more about spiders and less about baths and twins.

Jeremy James sat down on the lavatory again, legs dangling and lips pouting. What was the use of being a hero if nobody was interested? He glanced sadly down at the scene of his heroism – and his glance got stuck into a long and disbelieving stare: there, on the edge of the plughole, looking a little damp and dazed and drippy, was the ghost of the drowned spider.

Jeremy James leapt off the lavatory as if it had been a pincushion. 'Mummy!' he cried.

'What is it?' asked Mummy from one of the bedrooms.

'There's a spider in the bath!' cried Jeremy James.

'I thought you'd killed it,' said Mummy, now on the landing.

Jeremy James unlocked the bathroom door, and Mummy came in.

'Ugh!' she said. 'What a monster!'

'I did kill it,' said Jeremy James, 'but it must have unkilled itself.'

'Well, this is what we do with spiders,' said Mummy. On the bathroom shelf, next to the tooth-brush stand, was the mouthwash glass, which Mummy picked up in her right hand. With her left, she tore off a sheet of toilet paper. 'Now watch carefully,' she said.

Then she bent over the bath, and put the glass upside down round the spider. She slid the sheet of paper under the glass and under the spider, turned the glass the right way up, and plop! There was the spider sitting at the bottom of the glass.

'He doesn't look quite so big now, does he?' said Mummy, holding the glass so that Jeremy James could see.

In fact the spider seemed quite small and silly, sitting there looking out at Jeremy James looking in.

'What shall we do with him?' asked Mummy.

'Can we throw him out of the window?' suggested Jeremy James.

'Good idea,' said Mummy.

She opened the window, leaned out, and with a flick of her wrist sent the spider diving down to the lawn below. Then she showed Jeremy James the empty glass, which she washed out and replaced on the bathroom shelf.

'Can spiders fly?' asked Jeremy James.

'Yes,' said Mummy. 'But only downwards.

Mummy left the bathroom, and Jeremy James perched on the lavatory again. It was amazing how simple things were when Mummy did them. He looked all round the bathroom, hoping to see another spider so that he could do the trick with the glass and paper. But there wasn't a spider to be seen.

There was just one thing about Mummy's trick that slightly worried Jeremy James. It was nothing very important, but when a little later he cleaned his teeth, he rinsed his mouth with water straight from the tap. He didn't really need a glass for that anyway.

CHAPTER FOUR

Campers

Mummy was changing Christopher's nappy when the front doorbell rang.

'Jeremy James, would you please see who it is!' called Mummy from upstairs, and Jeremy James stood on tiptoe to open the front door. Standing on the step were Mrs Smyth-Fortescue from next door, and her son Timothy, who was a year older than Jeremy James and knew all about everything.

'Hello, Jeremy,' said Mrs Smyth-Fortescue, who never called him Jeremy *James*. 'Is your Mummy in?'

'Yes, Mrs Smyth-Forciture,' said Jeremy James, who never said Smyth-*Fortescue*, 'but Christopher's just done a pong.'

'Ah, she's changing him, is she?' asked Mrs Smyth-Fortescue.

'No,' said Jeremy James, 'I think she's going to keep him.'

Mummy came down the stairs. 'Hello, Mrs Smyth-Fortescue,' she said. 'Won't you come in?'

'No, we can't stop,' said Mrs Smyth-Fortescue. 'We just popped round to see if Jeremy would like to spend the night in Timothy's new tent. We bought it yesterday – frightfully expensive, but his old one was falling to bits, and he did so want this new one. It's the best on the market.'

'I'm sure he'd like to,' said Mummy.

'Jeremy's such good company for Timothy,' said Mrs Smyth-Fortescue. 'And they get on so nicely together.'

Timothy looked at Jeremy James and held his nose, and Jeremy James poked out his tongue at Timothy.

'Would you like that, Jeremy James?' asked Mummy.

'Ugh . . . hmmph . . . well . . .' said Jeremy James.

'Timothy doesn't want to sleep there on his own,' said Mrs Smyth-Fortescue, 'and I'm . . . well, ha ha . . . a little past such things, you know. My husband would keep Timothy company, but he's away on business. In America this time. Such a bore.'

'You'd love to sleep in Timothy's tent, wouldn't you, Jeremy James?' asked Mummy.

'Hmmph . . . well . . . ugh . . .' said Jeremy James.

'Oh good, I'm so glad,' said Mrs Smyth-Fortescue. 'Then that's settled. The tent's already up in the back garden, and I'll cook them a lovely barbecue supper. Do you like sausages, Jeremy?'

'Well, yes,' said Jeremy James.

'And baked beans and chips?'

Jeremy James did like baked beans and chips, and he liked sausages, and he liked the idea of sleeping in a tent. It was just a pity that Timothy would have to be there as well.

'Good,' said Mrs Smyth-Fortescue. 'We'll see you later, Jeremy.'

'Yes, Mrs Smyth-Torcyfue,' said Jeremy James.

'Big pong,' said Timothy.

'And so are you,' said Jeremy James.

The new tent was a beauty. It was high enough for the boys to stand in, and apart from the two airbeds, one on either side of the central pole, there was even room for a little table and two little chairs. And here they sat as Mrs Smyth-Fortescue served them with sausages, baked beans and chips, Coca-Cola and ice cream. She left them gobbling like a couple of starved turkeys, and for minutes on end there was no sound but contented munching, slurping and burping.

When eventually they had finished, Jeremy James put his dessert plate on his dinner plate, and his glass on his dessert plate, and sat back feeling rather pleased with life.

'You've never been camping before!' said Timothy.

Jeremy James felt slightly less pleased with life. 'Hmmph!' he said.

'Real campers don't put their dishes like that,' said Timothy. 'Anybody who knows anything about camping knows you don't put dishes like that!'

'Well, how do you put dishes, then?' asked Jeremy James.

'You leave them – like this,' said Timothy, indicating his own dishes spread out over the table.

'My mummy says you should put your dishes like this!' said Jeremy James, indicating his neat little pile.

'Then your mummy doesn't know anything about camping either,' said Timothy.

Just then Mrs Smyth-Fortescue arrived to collect the dirty dishes. 'Oh, what a good boy, Jeremy,' she said. 'Piling up your dishes so nicely.'

'My mother's never been camping either,' said Timothy, when Mrs Smyth-Fortescue had gone. 'It's only men who know about camping.'

'You're not a man,' said Jeremy James.

'I will be soon,' said Timothy. 'Much sooner than you.'

'Well, if you're such a man,' said Jeremy James, 'why were you scared to sleep in the tent on your own?'

'Scared?' said Timothy. '*Scared???* Me??? I'll show you who's scared!'

Whereupon he hurled himself at Jeremy James, and as he was much bigger and heavier, it was not long before he was sitting on Jeremy James's chest, with his knees pinning Jeremy James's arms to the ground.

'Now who's scared?' asked Timothy, scowling down.

'Just because you're bigger than me,' said Jeremy James, 'it doesn't prove you're not . . . ouch!'

Timothy had leaned forward, squashing Jeremy James's head with his chest.

'Having a nice game, dears?' came the voice of Mrs Smyth-Fortescue. 'You'd better go to the bathroom now, before it gets really dark. Timothy, get off Jeremy.'

'Can't,' said Timothy.

'Come along, Jeremy,' said Mrs Smyth-Fortescue. 'Let Timothy get off now.'

Eventually Mrs Smyth-Fortescue made Jeremy James let go of Timothy's knees with his arms, and release Timothy's bottom from his chest, and the two boys went to the house to wash their hands and faces, and clean their teeth. But Timothy didn't wash and didn't clean his teeth, because he said campers never did.

By the time they were tucked up in bed, the night was as black as Timothy's knees. Mrs Smyth-Fortescue had left them a torch which Timothy said only he should have, because he was the one that knew about camping. He shone it a few times in Jeremy James's eyes, but then he began to shine it round the tent, and the beam came to rest on the door-flap. 'Do you think a lion could get through the door?' he asked.

'I expect so,' said Jeremy James. 'Your mother got in, didn't she?'

'My mother's not a lion,' said Timothy.

'She's the same size as a lion,' said Jeremy James. 'But a bit fatter.'

There was a moment's silence. The torch continued to shine on the flap.

'A ghost could get in, too,' said Timothy.

'Ghosts can get in anywhere,' said Jeremy James. 'Ghosts can even get into your bedroom. And so can spiders.'

'Ugh!' said Timothy.

There was a noise outside the tent – a padding noise.

'What's that?' came Timothy's terrified whisper.

'I don't know,' whispered Jeremy James. 'Put the light out, so it won't know we're here!'

Timothy switched off the torch. There was more padding, then a snuffle-whiffle-snort, then silence. Then more silence.

'Has it gone?' whispered Timothy.

'Don't know,' whispered Jeremy James.

More silence. No more padding. No more snuffles. WHOO WHOO!

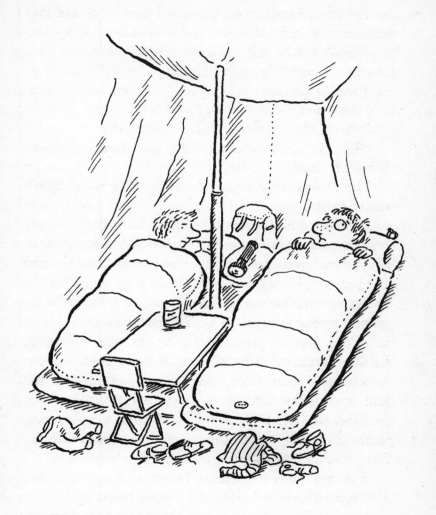

'W . . . w . . . wa . . . what's that?' Timothy's voice came out in a hoarse wobble.

'That's an owl,' said Jeremy James. 'No need to be scared of an owl!'

WHOO WHOO! WHOO WHOO!

'S . . . sou . . . sounds like a g . . . gug . . . ghost to me,' said Timothy.

'Ghosts say BOO, not WHOO,' said Jeremy James.

'S . . . s . . . some gug . . . gug . . . ghosts s . . . say WHOO!' said Timothy.

But boo-saying and whoo-saying ghosts didn't really matter any more to Jeremy James. The weight of the sausages, beans and chips had begun to shift from his tummy to his eyes, and when his eyes closed, his ears closed, too. Only his imagination stayed awake, supplying him with dreams of Mrs Smyth-Fortescue roaring on all fours, and of himself being pinned to the ground by a string of sausages.

When Jeremy James woke up the next morning, he was surrounded by a glow of orange and green, which he soon realized was the sun shining into the tent and on to the grass. The other thing he soon realized was that Timothy's bed and sleeping bag were still there, and Timothy's clothes were still there, but Timothy himself was most definitely not there.

Perhaps, thought Jeremy James with a little smile, a lion had gobbled Timothy up in the night. Or a ghost might have taken him off to the Land of Shivers. Anyway he had better tell Mrs Smyth-Fortescue. He wasn't sure whether Mrs Smyth-Fortescue would be glad or sorry that Timothy had disappeared, but she would certainly want to know.

Jeremy James stepped out of the tent and on to the lawn.

'Hello, Jeremy!' called Mrs Smyth-Fortescue through the open kitchen window. 'Did you sleep well?'

'Yes, thank you, Mrs Smyth-Forkystew,' said Jeremy James.

'I suppose Timothy's still asleep,' she said.

'I don't know,' said Jeremy James.

'You don't know?' said Mrs Smyth-Fortescue.

'Well, he's not there,' said Jeremy James.

'Not there?' echoed Mrs Smyth-Fortescue. 'Then where is he?'

'Well, we did hear a lion in the night,' said Jeremy James, 'so with a bit of luck . . .'

'Let's see if he's in his bedroom,' said Mrs Smyth-Fortescue.

So Jeremy James entered the house, and he and Mrs Smyth-Fortescue went upstairs to Timothy's bedroom. And there on the bed, totally uneaten and very asleep, lay Timothy.

'Wake up, dear!' said Mrs Smyth-Fortescue. 'Timothy, wake up!'

Timothy woke up. His eyes woke up first, and then his brain woke up second, and he sat up in surprise at the sight of his mother and Jeremy James.

'What are you doing here, dear?' asked Mrs

Smyth-Fortescue. 'You were supposed to be in the tent with Jeremy.'

'Oh . . . ugh . . . um . . . er . . .' said Timothy.

'What was that, dear?' said Mrs Smyth-Fortescue.

'Um . . . ugh . . .' said Timothy.

'Why aren't you in the tent, dear?' asked Mrs Smyth-Fortescue.

Timothy looked hard at the wall. Then he looked at the floor. And then at the bed.

'Um . . . I had a tummy ache. That's it, I had a tummy ache in the night. I had a tummy ache, so I had to come in.'

'Oh, what a shame,' said Mrs Smyth-Fortescue. 'It must have been all those sausages and beans. What a pity! And you were so looking forward to sleeping in the tent, weren't you, darling?'

'Yes, I was,' said Timothy. 'Only I had a tummy ache.'

'Well, it was very brave and sensible of you to come back here, then, dear,' said Mrs Smyth-Fortescue.

'Yes, I know,' said Timothy. 'I came back because I had a tummy ache.'

Timothy's tummy ache didn't stop him from eating a large breakfast of cornflakes, egg and bacon, and toast and marmalade. Jeremy James (who also had a large breakfast) did suggest to Timothy that perhaps people with tummy aches shouldn't be able to eat such large breakfasts, but Timothy said all campers had large breakfasts, and if Jeremy James had been a *real* camper, he'd have known that.

'A real camper,' said Jeremy James, with his mouth full of toast and marmalade, 'would know an owl isn't a ghost, and a real camper wouldn't get tummy ache in the night, and a real camper . . . a *real* camper . . .' continued Jeremy James, looking straight at Timothy, 'a *really* real camper wouldn't go to bed in his bedroom.'

Timothy munched his toast and marmalade, and for once he didn't say a word.

CHAPTER FIVE

Small Talk

There was a new arrival at the house. Jeremy James thought it was a marvellous new toy, Mummy thought it was very useful, and Daddy thought it was a worple worple nuisance. It was called a telephone.

One of the first calls was for Daddy, who was in the bath at the time. With the bath towel draped round his dripping body, he came paddling downstairs, arriving just as Mummy put the phone down.

'He'll ring back in half an hour,' said Mummy.

In fact he rang back in a quarter of an hour, which brought Daddy paddle-dripping down again. That was the first time Daddy called the phone a worple worple nuisance.

Jeremy James listened while Mummy rang a shop, but nothing special happened. She asked when they were open, was told the answer, and rang off. But Daddy's telephoning was rather different.

'I'll save myself a trip into town,' said Daddy. 'I'll ring the Post Office and find out the cost of an airmail letter to America.'

'Can I do the number, please, Daddy?' asked Jeremy James.

'Why not?' said Daddy. 'Let's have your finger. Now, press 7–4–4–3–1–1.'

With the receiver at his ear, Jeremy James listened to the whirring of the numbers, and when he had finished he could hear a brrr brrr sound at the other end.

'I'd better take it now,' said Daddy.

Jeremy James heard someone say, 'Hello', and then Daddy said: 'Good morning. Could you please tell me the cost of an airmail letter to America?'

The voice at the other end said something indistinct, and then Daddy said: 'Sorry, I must have got a wrong number,' and put the phone down. 'You must have done it wrong,' Daddy said to Jeremy James, and so Daddy pressed the numbers himself, got the same person again, and this time said he was extremely sorry. Then he looked in the phone book and found he'd chosen the number above the one he ought to have chosen. With the new number he got through to the Post Office, and was told he needed 'Enquiries'. 'Ah,' said Daddy, 'now we're getting somewhere!'

But 'Enquiries' said he needed 'Counter Services', and from 'Counter Services' there was nothing but brrr brrr.

'Probably gone for coffee,' said Daddy, putting the phone down with a bang and a tinkle.

'Or having a bath,' said Mummy.

That was the second time Daddy called the phone a worple worple nuisance.

Jeremy James wondered how people could make themselves small enough to get inside the phone, but Daddy explained that they didn't. They just sent their voices down the wire. Jeremy James pointed out that voices didn't have legs, and Daddy explained that they didn't need legs, because it was just a matter of soundwaves being what's-a-named into thingamies. Jeremy James didn't understand the what's-a-names or the thingamies, and so Daddy said: 'Well, that's how it is,' and so that was how it was.

What Jeremy James really wanted, far more than explanations of what's-a-names and thingamies, was the chance to make a phone call of his own. His chance came that same afternoon, when Daddy had gone to the Post Office to find out the cost of an airmail letter to America. Mummy and the twins were having a nap, and Jeremy James was supposed to be playing with his trains or his space machine or his farmyard. Of course, Mummy and Daddy had said he shouldn't touch the telephone, but what harm could come if he was careful not to drop it? And he would be *very* careful. He would hold the telephone as carefully as he would hold Christopher or Jennifer or a piece of chocolate.

Jeremy James picked up the telephone, which purred like a pussy-cat. He pressed a number. There was the same whirring sound as before. He pressed another number – and another, and another, and another, until . . . brrr brrr, brrr brrr. Jeremy James smiled with pleasure and excitement. Would it be Mummy's shop, or the Post Office, or . . .

'Hello,' said an elderly lady's voice at the other end.

'Hello,' said Jeremy James.

'Who is it?' asked the lady.

'It's me,' said Jeremy James.

'Who's me?' asked the lady.

'Jeremy James,' said Jeremy James.

'Who do you want to speak to, Jeremy James?' asked the lady.

'Well, you, if you don't mind,' said Jeremy James.

'Me?' said the lady. 'No, I don't mind – if you're sure it's me you want to speak to.'

'Quite sure,' said Jeremy James. 'I've just pressed your numbers.'

'Ah,' said the lady, 'that must be why my telephone rang.'

'It's lucky you answered it,' said Jeremy James.

'Why's that?' asked the lady.

'Because if you hadn't,' said Jeremy James, 'I wouldn't have been able to speak to you.'

'That's true,' said the lady. 'Now tell me, Jeremy James, what have you been doing with yourself?'

'Well, Daddy's out and Mummy and the twins are asleep, so I'm all on my own with boring trains and things,' said Jeremy James. 'What have *you* been doing?'

'I'm all on my own, too,' said the lady. 'So I was

knitting some clothes for my grandchildren.'

'Knitting!' cried Jeremy James. 'That's even more boring than trains!'

'There's not much else for me to do,' said the lady.

'No, there's not much else for me to do either,' said Jeremy James. 'Are your grandchildren asleep, too?'

'Oh no, they don't live here,' said the lady. 'I live alone.'

'Haven't you got a husband?' asked Jeremy James.

There was a little stretch of silence at the other end of the wire, and then the lady told Jeremy James that her husband had died six months ago. Her voice seemed suddenly to have a sort of knot tied in it. Jeremy James said he was sorry her husband had died, because that meant her husband wouldn't come back, would he?

'No, he won't come back,' said the lady sadly. 'And that's why I have to live alone.'

'Can I come and visit you one day?' asked Jeremy James.

'That would be lovely,' said the lady, 'but you don't know where I live, do you?'

'I could walk along the telephone wire,' said Jeremy James.

'I think it might be easier if I told you my name and address,' said the lady. 'Then perhaps your Mummy and Daddy could bring you for tea one day.'

Then she told Jeremy James her name, which was Mrs Small, and her address, which was 4 Silver Street, Netherton, Carlisle. Jeremy James repeated it several times so that he wouldn't forget it.

'Now, can you tell me your address?' asked the lady, and when Jeremy James told her, she let out a loud gasp. 'You're right down in the south!' she said. 'And I'm right up in the north! Oh dear, this call is going to cost you a lot of money!'

'No, it doesn't cost anything,' said Jeremy James. 'I just picked the phone up and pressed the numbers.'

'I'm afraid it's your daddy who'll have to pay,' said the lady, 'and he won't be very pleased. We'd better ring off, Jeremy James – but thank you for a really lovely chat.'

They said goodbye to each other, then there was

a click and the pussy-cat noise, which meant they couldn't talk any more.

Two days later, the front doorbell rang, and standing on the step was the postman with a big brown parcel for Jeremy James.

Mummy brought the parcel into the living room, and helped Jeremy James untie the string. Inside the brown paper was a box, and inside the box was . . .

'It's a walkie-talkie!' said Jeremy James.

'So it is!' said Mummy. 'Now who could have sent you that? Ah, there's a card.'

Jeremy James opened the card, and Mummy read it out to him:

> *'I hope that you'll be pleased to get*
> *This little walkie-talkie set.*
> *Perhaps when to your friends you call,*
> *You'll sometimes think of Mrs Small.'*

'Who's Mrs Small?' asked Mummy.

'She's the lady I spoke to on the telephone,' said Jeremy James.

'When was that?' asked Mummy.

'When you and the twins were asleep,' said Jeremy James.

'Oh, it was a wrong number, was it?' said Mummy. 'Good heavens, look at the address! Carlisle! That's a long way to dial a wrong number. How did she know your name and address, then, Jeremy James?'

'I told her,' said Jeremy James. 'We had a little chat.'

'Ah well,' said Mummy. 'I'm glad *we* shan't have to pay for your little chat!'

'Hmmph,' said Jeremy James, and buried his nose in the parcel.

CHAPTER SIX

The Gerbil

Richard was one of Jeremy James's best friends. He was a fat boy with a round red face, a round red mother, a tall thin father, and a short thin grandmother. They all lived across the road, down the end of the street, and round the corner at No 24. Sometimes Richard came to play with Jeremy James, and sometimes Jeremy James went to play with Richard. On this particular day it was Jeremy James who went to Richard.

'Come and see what I've got!' said Richard, his apple cheeks shining with pleasure.

Up to his room they went, and there on a table next to the wardrobe was a large white cage. Inside the cage, digging its way through a pile of sawdust and shredded paper was . . .

'It's a mouse!' said Jeremy James.

'No it's not,' said Richard. 'It's a gerbil.'

'A whattle?'

'A gerbil!' said Richard. 'It's just like a mouse, only different. Isn't it great!'

'Yes,' said Jeremy James. 'I wish I had one. What's it called?'

'Jerry,' said Richard. 'Or if it's a girl, Jenny.'

'My sister's Jenny,' said Jeremy James, 'only I'd sooner have a gerbil.'

'Would you like to hold it?' asked Richard.

'Oh!' said Jeremy James. 'Could I?'

'Yes,' said Richard. 'It's lovely to hold.'

Richard undid the hook on the door and reached into the cage.

'Come on, Jerry,' he said. 'This way.'

And when he turned towards Jeremy James, there was the gerbil cupped in the palm of his right hand, while his left hand gently stroked the little brown head.

'Now hold him firmly,' said Richard, 'but not too tight or you'll squash him.'

'All right,' said Jeremy James.

He held out his hand, and gave a little squeak of excitement as Richard gently lowered the gerbil on to his palm. It was the tingliest feeling. The little furry body nestled in his fingers, and he could feel its tiny movements as it breathed and tried to wriggle. Jeremy James found himself going goose-pimply all over.

'Nice, isn't it?' said Richard.

'Yes,' said Jeremy James. 'I wish *I* had a gerbil.'

'Richard!' It was the voice of Richard's mother from downstairs. 'Gran wants you!'

'She would!' said Richard. 'She always wants me

to do things when I'm doing other things. Hold Jerry; I'll be back in a minute.'

He clumped downstairs, and soon clumped upstairs again with the news that Gran wanted him to go to the library.

'Will you come with me?' he asked.

'All right,' said Jeremy James. 'Can I bring Jerry?'

'So long as you hold him tight,' said Richard. 'But not too tight.'

Off they went, with Richard holding a bag full of books, and Jeremy James holding a hand full of gerbil. When they reached the library, Richard handed the books to a lady at the counter, and then gave her a list of the new books Gran wanted. The librarian smiled at the two boys, and went to fetch the new books.

'I don't know why Gran wants all these books,' said Richard. 'She never reads them, 'cos she's always asleep. The only time she isn't asleep is when she's making me do things for her.'

'We've got a lot of books at home,' said Jeremy James. 'I think Mummy uses them to trap dust.'

As he spoke, Jeremy James's mind wandered to the books in the living room, and so he forgot to send certain important messages to his fingers. The fingers loosened their grip on the gerbil inside them, and wriggle, squeeze, plop, scurry – away it scampered across the library floor.

'Oh dear!' said Jeremy James.

'What's the matter?' asked Richard.

'There goes Jerry!' said Jeremy James.

With mouths gaping like cage doors, the boys watched the gerbil disappear into the reading room.

'We'd better go and get him,' said Richard, 'before someone treads on him.'

They headed towards the reading room, but before they had even reached the door, there was a terrified scream from within.

'Aaaaaaaargh! It's a mouse!'

Then there came a chorus of screams, chairs went flying, one woman clambered on to a table, another ran howling out of the room, and an elderly man with a pointed moustache started waving his walking stick in the air and shouting: 'Where is it? Where's the brute?'

By the time Richard and Jeremy James had timidly crept through the doorway, two more women had climbed on to the tables, and a third sat rigidly in her chair, crying, 'Save me! Save me!' Of Jerry there was no sign, which was a good thing because the owner of the moustache and stick was prowling round the room shouting: 'Where's the beast? I'll soon kill it!'

'Please don't kill him!' cried Richard. 'He's my pet gerbil!'

But nobody heard him above the screams of the women and the war cries of the moustache.

Jeremy James got down on his hands and knees. 'Jerry!' he cried. 'Come on, boy! Come on, Jerry! Or Jenny!'

Suddenly he saw a flash of brown in one corner

as the gerbil disappeared behind a bookcase. At that moment the moustache was in the opposite corner, shouting 'Come on out, you coward!'

'What's going on in here?' came a stern voice from the doorway. Jeremy James peeped out from under a table, and saw a man with a red face and bristles. 'What's all the fuss?' he was asking.

'Damned mouse on the rampage,' said the moustache.

'Save me! Save me!' cried the rigid woman.

'Help! Mouse! Help! Aaaaargh!' cried the other women.

'It's not a mouse,' said Richard, still standing by the door, 'it's my pet gerbil.' And he began to cry.

'I know where he is,' said Jeremy James from under his table. 'I'm sure I can get him out.'

The chief librarian looked redly and bristly down at Jeremy James. 'Get him out, then,' he ordered, 'and be quick about it.'

Jeremy James crawled swiftly across the room, like a cat in short trousers, and pressed himself up against the wall at the end of the bookcase. With one eye he could just see along the gap at the back, and nestling there in the shadow was the unmistakable shape of a tiny trembling gerbil.

By now the moustache had stopped waving the stick, the rigid woman had stopped asking to be saved, and the women on the tables had stopped screaming. As Jeremy James lay on the floor and squeezed his arm round behind the bookcase, the only sound to be heard was the quiet snuffle-snuffle of Richard.

'Got him!' said Jeremy James.

A sigh went round the reading room.

Jeremy James stood up, firmly holding the gerbil in one hand and stroking it with the other.

'Well done, lad,' said the moustache. 'Damned fine show!'

'Has it gone? Has it gone?' asked the rigid woman.

'It's only a little gerbil,' said Jeremy James, and just to show her how little it was, he stood beside her and took his stroking hand off Jerry's head.

The rigid woman took one look, gasped like a punctured tyre, slumped white-faced back in her chair, and fell fast asleep.

'Get out of here!' growled the bristly man. 'And don't you ever bring that animal in here again!'

Richard and Jeremy James left the reading room almost as fast as Jerry had entered it.

'Here are your books,' said the lady at the counter.

'Thank you,' said Richard, as he stuffed the books into his bag, and wobble-rushed out of the library as fast as his jellied legs could carry him. Jeremy James and the gerbil were right behind him.

A little old lady who was returning her books at the counter watched them go. 'How nice,' she said, 'to see children so eager to read.'

CHAPTER SEVEN

The Mess

'Just look at this mess!' said Mummy.

Jeremy James looked at the mess.

'Have you ever seen anything like it?' asked Mummy.

Jeremy James had often seen something like it. He saw something like it every day. The only time his room wasn't like it was when Mummy came in and made him un-mess it.

'I've lost count,' said Mummy, 'of the number of times I've tidied your room – and as fast as I tidy it, you untidy it. Look at your bed.'

Jeremy James looked at his bed.

'I don't mind the teddy,' said Mummy, 'but a racing car, a lorry, a gun, a book . . . and what's this sweet wrapper doing here?'

'Well, it's . . . sort of . . . lying there . . .' said Jeremy James.

'I don't know how you can sleep in the middle of all this,' said Mummy. 'Anyway, I want it all tidy. I've brought you a nice big box to put your toys in, and you can put the rubbish in this bin. Right?'

'Yes, Mummy,' said Jeremy James.

'And don't forget to do under the bed!'

'No, Mummy.'

Out went Mummy, and down sat Jeremy James. Tidy, tidy, tidy. What was the point in putting toys away? Toys were for playing with, not for putting away. It was only because grown-ups didn't play with toys that they wanted toys to be put away. Anyone who did play with toys knew that you couldn't play with toys that were stuck in boxes.

From downstairs came the faint sound of Mummy's voice: 'John, I do wish you'd keep your study tidier. I've never seen such a mess . . .'

Then a door shut, and Jeremy James couldn't hear any more.

Jeremy James looked at the box Mummy had brought. It was a big cardboard box with a picture of bananas on the side. You could sit in a box like that. You could make it into a boat, or tank, or plane. You could put sweets in it. Or even bananas. What a waste to put toys in a box like that!

Tidy, tidy, tidy. The bin was just a plain old tin bin. You could put it over your head, or bang it like a drum. Or put rubbish in it. What rubbish? The sweet wrapper perhaps – he wouldn't need that any more. It had once been a toffee – the best sort of toffee, hard and chewy and tooth-sticky. Now just a sweet memory.

Jeremy James carried the wrapper across to the bin, took careful aim, and let it fall. It floated sadly down, on to the carpet.

'Missed!' said Jeremy James.

He left it there. If it didn't want to go in, it didn't want to go in.

Jeremy James wandered across the room and looked out of the window. Perhaps there would be a message in the sky: Thou shalt not tidy or throw things away. But instead he saw the postman padding up the path. Could that mean another parcel from Mrs Small?

Jeremy James raced downstairs in time to see a letter squeeze through the flap and flop down into the hall. He picked it up. One flat letter. Too flat even to contain a stick of chewing gum.

Mummy emerged from the kitchen.

'There's a letter, Mummy,' said Jeremy James, holding it up and hoping Mummy would say: 'There's a good boy. Now you needn't bother with the tidying.'

'Thank you,' said Mummy, drying her hands on her apron. 'And how's the tidying going?'

'Well . . . hmmph . . .' said Jeremy James.

Mummy looked at the letter. 'Bill,' she said.

'Who's Bill?' asked Jeremy James.

'Electricity bill,' said Mummy.

And then there was a bang and a crash and a rude word from Daddy's study.

'What's Daddy doing?' asked Jeremy James.

'Tidying,' said Mummy. 'Off you go.'

Jeremy James dragged himself towards the stairs.

'Mummy,' he said, 'can I just have a little drink?'

'When you've put all your things away,' said Mummy, and went back into the kitchen.

Jeremy James was suddenly dying of thirst. Step by painful step he heaved himself up the stairs, like a cowboy heaving himself across the desert. Mummy would probably tell the cowboy: 'You can have your drink when you've put all the sand away.' Mummy was hard. It would serve Mummy right if she came upstairs and found Jeremy James all shrivelled up on the carpet.

Jeremy James lay down on the carpet, tongue hanging out, hand protecting his eyes from the burning sun and the circling vultures. Then with a shudder he gave one last gasp, and lay perfectly still.

But being dead wasn't much fun either, so he rolled over and over until he reached the bed. There were a lot of things under the bed – building blocks, cars, drawings, picture books. Under the bed was the best place for them. Under the bed they didn't cause any trouble at all. It was only when they came out from under the bed that they made a mess. But if they had to come out, then they had to come out, and so out they came.

A liquorice allsort packet looked interesting, but failed to rattle when shaken. An old toffee stuck to the bottom of a racing car might have been interesting once, but now with its coat of fluff and dust, it was more mucky than sucky. There was simply nothing but rubbish here, and what was the point of bringing rubbish out into the room. He could throw it all away, of course, but if he threw it away he wouldn't have it any more, and there was no point in *not* having things.

What was that glittering in the corner? Probably silver paper. It had better come out as well. Jeremy James snake-wiggled under the bed, reached out, and grasped a shape that was very familiar and very, very pleasing to the fingers. It was a solid square shape, with deep grooves all the way along and all the way across. It was a shape that brought happiness to the heart and water to the mouth. It was a bar-of-chocolate shape.

Jeremy James wiggle-snaked out from under the

bed to examine his treasure. Only in one corner had the silver paper been torn, and there the square of chocolate looked a little faded and dusty, but when he carefully peeled the foil away from the neighbouring square . . . well, it looked good enough to eat. And it was. And so was the square next to it. Would they all be as good?

It must have been at Christmas time, when he'd had so many nice things, and this one must have . . . would this square be all right, too? . . . must have slipped down between bed and wall . . . delicious . . . and hidden itself behind all the rubbish . . . amazing how it kept its flavour . . .

'Have you finished, Jeremy James?' came Mummy's voice from downstairs.

'Just a couple of squares to go!' called Jeremy James.

'What's that?' called Mummy.

'Oh!' said Jeremy James. 'Just a couple more things to put away!'

'Right, I'll be up in a minute!'

A minute! Time for action! Jeremy James put the remaining two squares in his mouth and scrunched them while he scooped up a pile of rubbish and dropped it in the box. On top of this pile of rubbish he dropped a second pile, and then a third. Next came the racing car, lorry, gun and book from the bed, more toys from the floor, the bedside table, the chair – everything piled onto the pile above the pile on the pile. With two seconds to go, as Mummy's footsteps creaked on the top stair, Jeremy James lifted up his bedside rug and spread it neatly over the bulging box.

'That's better,' said Mummy. 'Isn't that better, Jeremy James?'

'Yes, Mummy,' said Jeremy James.

'No rubbish, though?'

'No, Mummy.'

'Did you find any lost treasures?'

'Just a what's-a-name,' said Jeremy James.

'There you are,' said Mummy, 'it's worth keeping your room tidy.'

And she was so pleased with Jeremy James that she gave him three squares of chocolate. Unusually for him, Jeremy James had some difficulty forcing them down, and afterwards he needed two glasses of blackcurrant juice, because tidying was such thirsty work.

When Mummy had gone upstairs to vacuum Jeremy James's room, Daddy poked his head out of his study.

'Have you finished?' he asked Jeremy James.

'Yes,' said Jeremy James.

'So have I,' said Daddy. 'Want to look?'

Daddy's study was very tidy indeed. There were no papers or books or letters to be seen anywhere. On the desk was nothing but the typewriter, there was nothing on the floor, nothing on top of the filing cabinet, nothing on the window ledge.

'Pretty good, eh?' said Daddy. 'You want to know how it's done?'

'How?' asked Jeremy James.

Daddy marched to the built-in cupboard at the back of his study.

'Ta ra!' he sang, and flung open the cupboard door. And inside the cupboard was the biggest mess of papers, books and letters you ever saw.

'You see,' he said, 'these are the tricks you learn as you get older, Jeremy James. Out of sight, out of mind. But don't tell your mother.'

'I won't,' said Jeremy James.

CHAPTER EIGHT

Freezing

It was going to be a miserable afternoon. Uncle Jack and Aunt Janet had just arrived, with their daughter Melissa. Melissa was the same age as Jeremy James, and she was worse than tummy ache.

'Haven't you grown!' said Aunt Janet to Jeremy James.

'Yes,' said Jeremy James. It was difficult to think of any other answer.

'Oh, look at the twins!' she cried. 'They're *crawling*!'

Christopher and Jennifer were indeed scrabbling round the living room and giggling, but what was so special about that? If Jeremy James had crawled round giggling, would anyone have shrieked and clapped their hands? They'd probably have told him to stand up before his knees got dirty.

'Wait till you see them stand,' said Mummy.

At that very moment, Christopher seized hold of a chair leg, and slowly hauled himself to his feet, eyes shining with the effort and the triumph.

'Good! Good!' cried Aunt Janet, clapping again.

Jennifer crawled to Christopher, grabbed his leg, and pulled. Plonk. Down came Christopher, and his triumph crumpled into pain and shock. Out came the tears and the wailing cry. Jennifer sat and watched with an expression of amused interest.

'Jennifer, that's naughty!' said Mummy.

Jennifer smiled sweetly.

'Oh, aren't they gorgeous!' said Aunt Janet.

It was going to be a miserable afternoon.

Uncle Jack patted Jeremy James on the head. 'How's my favourite nephew, then?'

'Very well, thank you,' said Jeremy James.

Uncle Jack usually came up with a coin or two at the end of his visits, and so his questions were worth answering.

The pig-tailed Melissa stood clutching her dolly and watching the twins. In fact, everyone was watching the twins. This might be a good chance to escape before Mummy spoke the dreaded words: 'Jeremy James, why don't you go and play with Melissa?'

Jeremy James crept out of the living room, into the hall, up the stairs, and into his room. He was just about to close the door when Mummy's voice rang out:

'Jeremy James!'

'Yes, Mummy?'

'Where are you?'

'Here, Mummy!'

'Why don't you come and play with Melissa?'

It was a question which Jeremy James could have answered in some detail, but while he was still looking for the best way to start his list, Mummy spoke again:

'Melissa, dear, would you like to go up and play with Jeremy James?'

'No,' said Melissa.

'Good,' said Jeremy James.

'Up you go, then,' said Mummy.

'Come on, I'll take you,' said Aunt Janet. And up they came – Mummy, Aunt Janet, Melissa and Dolly.

'What a lovely tidy room!' said Aunt Janet.

Mummy smiled at Jeremy James, and Jeremy James grimaced at Mummy.

'Do you always keep it so tidy?' asked Aunt Janet.

'Only when Mummy makes me,' said Jeremy James.

'Now you'd better play in here till it stops raining,' said Mummy. 'So have a nice game.'

Mummy and Aunt Janet went downstairs again, leaving Jeremy James and Melissa to eye each other like cat and dog.

'What are we going to play?' asked Melissa.

'I don't know,' said Jeremy James. 'What about ludo?'

'I don't like ludo,' said Melissa.

'Do you like racing cars?' asked Jeremy James.

'No,' said Melissa.

'We could play cowboys,' said Jeremy James.

'I don't like cowboys,' said Melissa.

And Melissa didn't like guns or lorries or jungles or drawing or wrestling or spacecraft or anything in this whole wide world except . . .

'I like Freezing.'

'What's Freezing?'

'You hide something, and the other person has to find it, and you tell him if he's freezing, or cold, or warm, or hot.'

'Sounds silly to me.'

'That's the only game I like. If we can't play Freezing, I won't play anything, and I'll tell Mummy, so there.'

'Oh, all right,' said Jeremy James. 'Who's going to do the hiding?'

'You hide something, and I'll go out of the room till you're ready.'

Melissa and her dolly left the room. She did not close the door behind her, and Jeremy James could see her peeping through the crack between the hinges. He marched to the door and slammed it shut.

'Hope you got your nose caught!' he said. 'Rotten cheat!'

Now, the first thing to choose was the object to hide – something nice and small. Like a sweet wrapper. There was a sweet wrapper under his pillow. Where was the best place to hide it? On top of the wardrobe. She'd *never* think of looking up there.

'Are you ready yet?' asked Melissa from outside.

'No,' said Jeremy James.

He dragged his bedside chair across to the wardrobe, clambered up, put the sweet wrapper in the dust, got down, dragged the chair back to the bed, and sat in it.

'Ready!' he said.

In came Melissa.

'You'll never find it,' said Jeremy James.

'Oh yes I will,' said Melissa, and walked straight to the wardrobe. 'Am I warm?'

'Yes . . . well . . . sort of,' said Jeremy James.

'How warm?' asked Melissa.

'Very warm, I suppose,' said Jeremy James.

'Bring the chair here,' said Melissa.

'What for?' asked Jeremy James.

'Because,' said Melissa, 'I want to see what's on top of the wardrobe.'

'You cheated!' said Jeremy James. 'You were looking!'

'No I wasn't,' said Melissa. 'You closed the door, so how could I look?'

'You made a hole in it!'

'I didn't!'

'You did!'

'I didn't! Shall I tell you how I knew?'

'I don't care,' said Jeremy James. 'Rotten cheat!'

'I heard you moving the chair,' said Melissa.

'It's a silly game anyway,' said Jeremy James. 'I'm not playing silly games.'

'I bet I can hide something where you won't find it,' said Melissa.

'I bet you can't,' said Jeremy James.

'All right,' said Melissa, 'you go out of the room and close the door.'

Jeremy James went out of the room, and closed the door. Then he stood up against the door and put his ear close to it. Not a sound. He bent down to try and see underneath, but the carpet blocked his view. He looked for a hole or a crack, but there were no holes or cracks. All the same, he'd soon find whatever she hid wherever she hid it.

'Ready!' called Melissa.

In marched Jeremy James. Melissa was standing with her dolly beside the wardrobe. Jeremy James headed straight for the wardrobe and Melissa moved out of the way.

'Well?' asked Jeremy James.

'Freezing,' said Melissa.

Jeremy James walked confidently to the other side of the room where he had his box of toys. Melissa returned to the wardrobe.

'Freezing,' she said.

Jeremy James walked a little less confidently to his bed, and Melissa wandered over to the door.

'Freezing,' she said.

'Aha!' said Jeremy James. There was now only one side of the room where he hadn't been. He crossed to the door, and Melissa stepped aside and stood in front of the wardrobe again.

'Freezing,' she said.

'How can it be freezing?' said Jeremy James. 'I've been . . . ah!'

He had not yet tried the middle of the room, and hanging down from the ceiling was the lampshade.

'Clever,' said Jeremy James. 'But not clever enough.'

He stood below the lamp.

'Freezing,' said Melissa.

Jeremy James stood in the middle of the room and scratched his head. This was not so easy. If it wasn't on any side or in the middle, where could it be? Unless . . . could she have put it outside?

Melissa was still in front of the wardrobe, and beside the wardrobe was the window. Jeremy James took a cautious step towards the window, then looked inquiringly at Melissa.

'A tiny bit warmer,' she said.

He took another step.

'A tiny bit warmerer,' she said.

Jeremy James took two more steps, and Melissa moved aside.

'Colder,' she said.

Jeremy James frowned. How could it be colder when he'd actually gone nearer? Maybe she'd made a mistake. He went all the way to the window.

'Freezing,' she said.

Jeremy James was fed up. Wherever he went he was freezing, and even when he was warmer he was soon colder and it just didn't make sense.

'Give up?' asked Melissa.

'It's a stupid game,' said Jeremy James. 'I don't care where you've hidden whatever it is.'

'It's one of your little racing cars,' said Melissa.

'I couldn't care less,' said Jeremy James.

'Then I won't tell you where it is,' said Melissa.

'Where is it?' asked Jeremy James.

'It's in Dolly's knickers,' said Melissa, pulling Dolly's skirt up to reveal her triumph.

'That's not fair!' said Jeremy James.

'Yes it is,' said Melissa, 'and I told you you'd never find it.'

'I'm not playing any more stupid games!' said Jeremy James, and pulled his lorry out of the box and sent it hurtling across the room into the wall below the window.

When Mummy came to fetch them for tea, Melissa was quietly combing Dolly's hair, and Jeremy

James was quietly drawing a little girl. The little girl in his drawing was flat on her back with a big dagger in her chest.

'What good children,' said Mummy. 'Had a nice game, then?'

'Yes,' said Melissa.

'No,' said Jeremy James.

Uncle Jack, Aunt Janet, Melissa and Dolly finally left, in a flurry of kisses and heart-sinking promises to come again soon. It had indeed been a thoroughly miserable afternoon, but two bright things had come out of it. One was the shiny fifty-pence piece that Uncle Jack slipped into Jeremy James's hand as they said goodbye. Fifty pence was worth being miserable for. And the other consolation was the thought that it might be fun to have a game of Freezing with Timothy from next door. Especially if they each hid a packet of sweets and played finders keepers.

CHAPTER NINE

The Crooked House

Mummy had decided that the whole family should have their photograph taken. Mummy and Daddy themselves had, of course, taken lots of photographs – whole albums of them. Mummy was very good at photographing upwards – her photos were always full of huge expanses of sky, tree-tops, or the roofs of houses, and if they were taken indoors she was good at catching ceilings and the tops of walls. Then occasionally she would also manage to catch somebody's face, usually right down at the bottom of the picture.

Daddy, on the other hand, photographed downwards. He was a specialist in feet, lawns, roads and carpets. Legs and even bodies could often be seen in his pictures, but faces were a rarity. If he did photograph a face, it usually ended at the mouth or nose. You hardly ever saw a pair of eyes in one of Daddy's pictures.

And so Mummy persuaded Daddy to make an appointment with a Mr Pringle, who was a real photographer and could actually get faces into the middle of his pictures. He lived a little way out of town, but the Smyth-Fortescues from next door had been to him, and Mummy reckoned that if he could photograph Timothy, he could photograph anyone.

Mr Pringle had wavy grey hair and a smooth pink face, and he wore a mauve jacket. He didn't say 'photograph' but 'photogwaph', and he walked with a heavy limp, as if one of his legs was twice as heavy as the other. He lived in a tiny cottage, whose doorways were so low that Daddy had to duck his head to get through them. The little rooms were full of pictures and ornaments, and there seemed hardly enough space for anyone to sit down. Not that the family were invited to sit down – they simply passed through, on their way to what looked like a barn in the back garden. The barn was what Mr Pringle called his studio, and it was full of lights, pictures, screens and cameras.

'Have you ever been inside a studio before, Jewemy James?' asked Mr Pringle.

'I don't think so,' said Jeremy James. 'And why do you talk so funny?'

'Well,' said Mr Pringle, 'I can't pwonounce my 'r's. Some childwen can't pwonounce r either, but I suppose you can.'

'Yes,' said Jeremy James.

'Lucky you,' said Mr Pringle.

'And why do you walk so funny?' asked Jeremy James.

'Sh, Jeremy James,' said Mummy, her face going a little red.

'It's all wight,' said Mr Pringle. 'He's quite wight to ask. I can't walk pwoperly because I've lost a leg.'

'Does that mean your leg is dead?' asked Jeremy James. 'Or did you just drop it somewhere?'

Jeremy James had once met a lady who had lost her husband and son, and he'd spent hours looking for them till he was told that 'lost' meant 'dead'. Now he wasn't sure when lost meant dead and when lost meant lost (as in 'I've lost a piece of chocolate') – but apparently Mr Pringle's leg was neither dead lost nor lost lost, but had simply been taken away after an accident.

'Where did they put your leg after they'd taken it away?' asked Jeremy James.

'To tell you the twuth,' said Mr Pringle, 'I don't know. Maybe they buwied it.'

Jeremy James would have liked to ask more questions about the lost leg, but Mr Pringle now busied himself in the studio. He slid a white screen across the back of a platform at one end, then he placed two chairs on the platform for Mummy and Daddy to sit on. Mummy was to hold Christopher, Daddy was to hold Jennifer, and Jeremy James was to stand in between. It was all very simple, until Mr Pringle started messing about with the lights. He turned them on, he turned them off, he moved them here, he moved them there, he made them lighter, he made them darker, he put them lower, he put them

higher . . . and all the time he kept saying: 'We must get it wight, mustn't we?'

'But not,' said Daddy to Mummy, 'black and wight.'

Jeremy James decided that photography was boring. Jennifer decided it was funny (perhaps because of the silly faces Daddy was pulling), and Christopher decided it was the perfect moment to do his Number Two. There was a sudden loud and rather rude noise, he wriggled back stiffly in Mummy's arms, and the studio was soon filled with a smell that had nothing to do with photography.

'Oh dear,' said Mummy, 'I think I'd better change him, or we'll never be able to smile.'

Mr Pringle caught a whiff and swiftly opened the door for Mummy.

Jeremy James followed Mummy and Christopher out of the studio, but while they went on through the house, he decided to do a bit of exploring. He wandered round the side of the studio, and found himself in a strange little garden full of flowers and gnomes and toy animals. At the very top of this garden, up a crazy paving path, stood a tiny crooked house which looked as if it had come straight out of a book of fairy tales. It was painted in bright colours, and its roof, chimney, windows and door were all set at different angles. It was the kind of house you simply had to go and have a look at.

Jeremy James tried to peep through its windows, but they were covered on the inside with black blinds, so he couldn't see anything. Next he tried the door, and to his delight it opened. He looked inside, but it was still too dark for him to see anything.

'Is anybody there?' he asked.

Nobody said anything.

'Anybody at home?' asked Jeremy James.

Complete silence.

Witches lived in houses like these, so you had to be careful. It could be the house of the witch that took Mr Pringle's leg away after his accident. Mr Pringle might even have come here looking for his leg and not found it because it was too dark for him to find anything. Or because he was too frightened to look. After all, not everyone is brave enough actually to go *inside* a witch's house. Jeremy James wasn't even certain that *he* was brave enough.

'Are you sure you're not at home?' asked Jeremy James.

No reply.

If a witch was at home, she'd probably say, 'Come in, dear.' And if she was asleep, she would be snoring. Jeremy James stood still and quiet. Not a sound. He pushed the door open as wide as it could go. Still not a sound.

'I can see you,' he said. 'You're hiding behind the door!'

Not a murmur, not a movement.

Jeremy James took a deep breath, and stepped inside the crooked house. He stood there for a

moment, waiting to be bonked on the head, but nothing happened. In the light from the doorway he could now see some tables and stands with things hanging on them. No sign of a leg, but that could be hidden in the shadows. He needed more light. Jeremy James boldly marched to one of the blinds. It was attached by a simple loop on a hook, and in no time at all, Jeremy James had raised both blinds and the sunlight was streaming all over the crooked house. It revealed nothing but long strips of shiny film hanging on the stands, photographs on the walls, basins of water with papers in them . . . no witches, no gingerbread men, no toys, no magic potions, and no lost legs. It was all a big disappointment.

'Jeremy James!' That was Daddy's voice, calling

from the garden. Jeremy James walked out of the crooked house.

'Ah, there you are!' said Daddy. 'I thought you'd gone with Mummy. Nice little house that, isn't it?'

'No,' said Jeremy James. 'It's boring.'

'Anyway, come on,' said Daddy. 'Mr Pringle's waiting for us.'

And the 'photogwaphing' proved to be as boring as the rest of the afternoon.

A week later, Mr Pringle brought the photographs round to Mummy and Daddy. Even Jeremy James had to agree that they were beautiful pictures. Somehow everyone had managed to look happy, handsome and smart, and seeing those handsome happy faces, you would never have thought of moving lights, pooey nappies and yawning boredom.

'I'm glad you like them,' said Mr Pringle. 'You know, a tewwible thing happened that day you came.'

'What was that?' asked Daddy.

'Somebody bwoke into my dark woom. They let all the blinds up, and all my photogwaphs were wuined – absolutely wuined. A whole week's work destwoyed.'

'Oh dear,' said Mummy. 'Who would do an awful thing like that?'

'I expect it was childwen,' said Mr Pringle. 'They didn't take anything. Just wuined the photogwaphs.'

A thought struck Jeremy James. At the same time, the same thought struck Daddy.

'Mr Pringle,' said Daddy. 'Your dark room – it

isn't that little crooked house in the garden, is it?'

'That's wight,' said Mr Pringle.

'Oh!' said Daddy.

And 'Oh!' thought Jeremy James.

'In that case, Mr Pringle,' said Daddy, 'perhaps you and I could have a little chat.'

Daddy and Mr Pringle went out, with Daddy looking worried and Mr Pringle looking puzzled, and they left Jeremy James looking uncomfortable, and Mummy looking at the photographs.

'Mummy,' said Jeremy James. 'What's a dark woom?'

'A dark *room*,' said Mummy. 'It's a place where photographers develop their photographs. They make the film into photos.'

'Why is it dark?' asked Jeremy James.

'Because light ruins the film,' said Mummy.

'Oh!' said Jeremy James.

'Do you know something about Mr Pringle's dark room?' asked Mummy.

'Well,' said Jeremy James, 'I think I may have been there.'

Before Mummy could ask any more questions, Daddy came back with Mr Pringle, and Daddy was looking embarrassed, and Mr Pringle was looking pleased.

'Is everything all right?' asked Mummy.

'You might say,' said Daddy, 'that the answer is in the negative.'

When Mr Pringle had gone, Daddy explained to

Mummy that Jeremy James had unfortunately been exploring in Mr Pringle's garden, and he then explained to Jeremy James that other people's closed doors were best left closed.

'I was only looking for Mr Pringle's leg,' said Jeremy James.

Mummy and Daddy both agreed that Jeremy James couldn't have known what was behind the door, and maybe Mr Pringle should have kept it locked, knowing there were children about.

'Anyway,' said Daddy, 'let's have a good look at these photographs. Because believe me, they're worth their weight in gold.'

'How much did you give him?' asked Mummy.

Jeremy James gasped when he heard the sum.

'You could buy a million ice creams with that!' he cried.

'That,' said Daddy, 'is the price of development. His, and yours.'

CHAPTER TEN

Birthday Twins

Tomorrow would be the twins' first birthday.

'I wish,' said Jeremy James at the breakfast table, 'that I could have a gerbil for their birthday.'

'Why,' asked Daddy from behind the newspaper, 'should *you* have a gerbil for *their* birthday?'

'Well, Richard's got a gerbil,' said Jeremy James. 'And it runs round a wheel and it eats paper and it's clever and nice and I wish I could have a gerbil.'

'Yes, I understand that,' said Daddy. 'What I don't understand is why *you* should have a gerbil for the *twins*' birthday.'

'Because,' said Jeremy James, 'people give people presents on people's birthdays.'

Mummy explained to Jeremy James that it was only the people that had birthdays who were given presents. Jeremy James explained to Mummy that at the birthday parties he'd been to, *everybody* was given a present, and the present he would like to be given was a gerbil.

'And what present are you going to give the twins?' asked Mummy.

This was a problem that Jeremy James had been trying hard not to think about. The trouble was, his pocket money had all gone to the sweetshop, and Uncle Jack's fifty pence had gone the same way, and how do you get people presents if you haven't got any money?

Jeremy James put this question to Mummy and Daddy.

'It's a good question,' said Daddy.

Jeremy James was pleased that Daddy liked his question, and he waited for the answer. But the answer didn't come. Daddy simply put his eyes back on his newspaper and his lips back on his cup of tea. Daddy wasn't very good at solving problems anyway..

'Mummy,' said Jeremy James, 'if you hadn't got any money, how would you buy presents?'

'If I knew that I had to buy presents,' said Mummy, 'I'd make sure I saved some money for them. Instead of spending it all at the sweetshop.'

Mummy was good at solving problems. Only her solutions didn't always help Jeremy James.

Jeremy James decided to ask the twins for a solution, and the solution he had in mind seemed a rather clever one.

'You don't really want a birthday present, do you?' he said to Christopher, while Mummy was bathing Jennifer.

'Hihihi!' gurgled Christopher, standing up in his cot and shaking the sides.

'Say no,' said Jeremy James.

'Hihihi!' said Christopher.

'Not hihihi,' said Jeremy James. 'No. Say no. *No-o-o.*'

'Hihihi,' said Christopher.

Christopher was just like Daddy when it came to solving problems.

Ten minutes later, when Mummy was bathing Christopher, Jeremy James put his suggestion to Jennifer.

'You don't want a birthday present, do you?' he said. 'Just say no.'

'Ball,' said Jennifer.

'What?' said Jeremy James.

'Ball,' said Jennifer. 'Boo ... Jem Jem ... Wiffer...'

'No,' said Jeremy James. 'Say no.'

Jennifer laughed. 'Jem Jem!' she said. 'Wiffer... ball ... Jeffer ... boo.'

Jennifer was just like Mummy when it came to solving problems.

In the course of the morning, Jeremy James had two more ideas about how to escape from present-buying. The first was to fall ill. Nobody can buy presents when they're ill. But the only time he'd been ill, it had been through eating too many liquorice allsorts, and to eat too many liquorice allsorts he would first of all need to *have* too many liquorice allsorts, and in his present state of coinlessness he could not even afford one liquorice allsort let alone too many.

The second idea seemed more possible. He explained it to Mummy and Daddy at lunch.

'If you give me the gerbil as my present *before* the twins' birthday,' he said, '*I* could give it to *them* as *their* present, couldn't I?'

'What gerbil?' asked Daddy.

The idea began to seem less possible.

'What would Christopher and Jennifer do with a gerbil?' asked Mummy.

The idea didn't seem possible at all.

In the course of the afternoon, Jeremy James had no further ideas except the idea that other people's birthdays were a bad idea.

At tea Mummy saw the worried expression on Jeremy James's face and she told him that he didn't really have to buy the twins a present at all. She said they were too young to understand about birthdays anyway. But Mummy was always saying Jeremy James was too young to understand things, and he knew that he wasn't. He understood everything, except why grown-ups thought children were too young to understand things they did understand or would understand if the things were properly explained. The twins certainly understood about birthdays, and if they wanted a present and he didn't buy them a present, they certainly wouldn't buy *him* a present when it was *his* birthday.

No idea came into Jeremy James's head that evening (perhaps because he was busy watching a film). And no ideas came into his head that night (perhaps because he was busy sleeping). But the following morning, when he woke up, there in his brain lay the answer, and it was so simple that he wondered why he hadn't thought of it before. Mummy had been completely wrong. Not only did the twins understand about birthdays, but they'd even solved Jeremy James's problem for him.

With a little giggle of excitement, Jeremy James leapt out of bed, and a moment later there was a sound rather like a building falling down. This was followed by a good deal of banging and scraping, and when Mummy poked her nose through the door to see what was going on, she saw Jeremy James sitting beside his upside-down toy box, surrounded by toys.

'What on earth are you doing?' she asked.

Jeremy James thought for a moment.

'Tidying,' he said.

'Ah,' said Mummy. 'Good.' And off she went to prepare breakfast.

By the time breakfast was ready, Jeremy James had finished banging and scraping, and he had also finished a long session of rustling. His smile had spread all over his face much as his toys had spread all over the floor, because he had found what he had been looking for. When he went downstairs, he felt light enough to fly. It was almost worth having problems just for the pleasure of finding the solutions.

When Mummy and Daddy had dressed Christopher and Jennifer in their new birthday clothes and had placed their new giant teddy bears in their arms, Jeremy James raced to his room and returned with two parcels. One of them was small and round and wrapped in an old paper bag. The other was large and square and wrapped in two old paper bags.

'Boo!' said Jennifer, as she took the bags off her present. 'Jeffer . . . boo!' And a 'boo' it was. One of Jeremy James's old picture books which had been buried at the bottom of his toy box.

'Hihihi!' said Christopher, as he took the paper bag off his present.

'Wiffer . . . ball!' cried Jennifer, glancing across at her brother. And a ball it was. A bouncy rubber ball which Jeremy James sometimes played with in the garden. It was a ball he would rather like to

play with again, so perhaps he might borrow it from Christopher later on.

'Very nice presents,' said Mummy.

'Well done, Jeremy James,' said Daddy.

'It's just what they wanted,' said Jeremy James. 'They told me when I asked them.'

'Talking of what people want,' said Daddy, 'there's something up in our bedroom that might interest you, Jeremy James.'

Jeremy James broke the world record for up-the-stairs-and-into-the-bedroom. On the dressing table was a large cage of glass and metal, and inside it was a wheel. Near the wheel was a ladder, and near the ladder was a swing. And near the swing was a bowl of water, and near the bowl of water was a pile of sawdust. And in the sawdust, huddled together and fast asleep, were the tiny furry bodies of ... *two gerbils*!

Jeremy James let out a whoop that would have turned an oak tree into sawdust. *Two gerbils*!

'We thought one would be lonely on its own,' said Daddy from the bedroom doorway. 'Happy Unbirthday, Jeremy James.'

'*Two gerbils*!' cried Jeremy James for the third time.

'What are you going to call them, then?' asked Mummy from behind Daddy.

Jeremy James knew straight away what the gerbils were going to be called.

'Wiffer and Jeffer,' he said.

Mummy and Daddy laughed.

'Why Wiffer and Jeffer?' asked Daddy.

'Because,' said Jeremy James, 'they're twins and they're clever and nice and thank you and Richard's only got one gerbil and Wiffer and Jeffer are the best present in the whole world . . .'

There was no doubt that birthdays were a good idea after all. And so were twins.

Do Goldfish
Play the
Violin?

For my brother Peter,
to read to Robin and Ian

Contents

CHAPTER ONE

Monday Morning

Jeremy James watched in amazement as his bowl of cornflakes slid across the table.

Swish, crash, tinkle, smash, wah!

These were the sounds made by the breakfast things as they all fell from the table to the floor – except 'wah!' which was the sound made by Christopher as the cornflake packet landed on his head.

The breakfast things had fallen to the floor because of Jennifer's right hand, right leg, and left leg. Her right hand had caught hold of the table cloth, and her right leg and left leg had carried her across the room while she was still holding the cloth. And so down came the cloth and cornflakes and all.

'Oh, you naughty girl,' said Jeremy James.

'Oh, you naughty, naughty girl!' cried Mummy, and gave Jennifer a smack on the bottom. Jennifer smiled sweetly, pointed to the collection of cups and cornflakes, milk and marmalade, bowls and butter all over the floor, and said, 'Mess!'

Mummy set to work cleaning up the mess, Jeremy James kissed Christopher's head better, and Daddy came downstairs with his razor in his hand and a cut on his chin.

'What happened?' he asked.

'Jennifer pulled the cloth off,' said Mummy.

'You naughty girl,' said Daddy.

'Nor-ty,' said Jennifer. 'Nor-ty.'

The twins were a menace. Now that they could walk, they were everywhere. Daddy had put a gate at the top of the stairs to make sure they didn't fall down. Only Daddy had forgotten about the gate one night, and *he* had fallen down. He had also bought a huge playpen to keep them fenced in, but they couldn't be fenced in all the time, and it was during the unfenced-in time that they were a menace. Jennifer was more of a menace than Christopher. She now waddled over to have a look at him.

'Wiffer cwy,' she said.

'Of course he's crying,' said Jeremy James. 'He got hit on the head by the cornflakes.'

Jennifer lifted the packet of cornflakes and smacked it hard. 'Nor-ty corflay!' she said, and laughed.

Daddy helped Mummy with the tidying, until he cut his finger on a broken saucer and went upstairs to get some plaster.

'Daddy blood!' said Jennifer.

'And it's your fault,' said Jeremy James.

'Nor-ty Jeffer,' said Jennifer.

'Any idea where the plaster is?' came Daddy's voice from upstairs.

'In the medicine cupboard,' called Mummy.

By the time Daddy had come downstairs again, with a plaster on his chin and on his finger, Mummy had reset the breakfast table, the twins were in their playpen, and Jeremy James was halfway through his toast and marmalade.

'What a start to the week!' said Daddy. 'Typical Monday morning.'

But worse was to follow. Daddy had to go out, and after breakfast Jeremy James wandered into his study to watch him getting things ready. It was always interesting to watch Daddy get things ready. First he had to find his papers, then his pen, his wallet, his cheque book, his what's-a-name (he could *never* find his what's-a-name), and finally his briefcase. It was Jeremy James who found the briefcase, which had somehow got wedged between the filing cabinet and the bookcase.

'Thanks, Jeremy James,' said Daddy. 'I really must get this place tidied up. Right, now we're all set. Where are the car keys?'

And that was when the trouble really started. They were not on his desk, they were not on the key hook, and they were not in his jacket pocket.

'Have you looked in your overcoat?' asked Mummy.

Daddy hadn't looked in his overcoat. But when he did look in his overcoat, there were no car keys.

'Have you looked in your trousers?' asked Jeremy James.

Daddy put his hands in his trouser pockets. No car keys.

Daddy went into his study, shouted 'Yaaaaaah-grrrrrraaaaaah!' very loudly, and hurled a bunch of papers all over the room. But even that didn't bring the keys out of hiding.

'I can't understand it!' Daddy howled. 'I had them yesterday! Things just disappear in this house.'

'They don't disappear,' said Mummy. 'You lose them. You should keep things tidier.'

'I don't lose them,' said Daddy. 'They move around.'

It occurred to Jeremy James that the keys might have moved around with Daddy.

'They might be in the medicine cupboard,' he suggested.

'Not likely,' said Daddy. 'Plaster goes in the medicine cupboard. And medicine.'

'And keys,' said Mummy, 'go on the key hook.'

Daddy went upstairs. The keys were not in the medicine cupboard.

'Have you looked in your other jackets and trousers?' asked Mummy.

While Mummy and Daddy searched jackets and trousers, Jeremy James searched Daddy's study again, but the keys had not fallen down between the filing cabinet and the bookcase, or under Daddy's desk, or inside his typewriter, or into his wastepaper basket. Nor had they been found in the other jackets and trousers.

'Just stop and think,' said Mummy. 'When did you have them last?'

Daddy stopped and thought. 'Yesterday, when I washed the car,' he said.

'And where did you put them?' asked Mummy.

'If I knew where I'd put them,' said Daddy, 'I'd know where to find them.'

'I know where Daddy sometimes puts the car keys,' said Jeremy James.

'Where?' asked Daddy.

'In the car,' said Jeremy James.

'Aha!' said Daddy. 'I didn't think of that.'

Out went Daddy to look in the car. And back came Daddy from looking in the car. The car was locked, and there were no keys in it.

'Well, you'll just have to take the spare keys,' said Mummy.

'I can't,' said Daddy.

'Why not?' asked Mummy.

'They're lost,' said Daddy.

Jeremy James wandered into the living room. That had been searched three or four times but had proved as keyless as all the other rooms. The keys had vanished and it looked as if they would never be unvanished.

'Jem Jem!' said Jennifer from the playpen.

'Hello,' said Jeremy James. 'You haven't seen Daddy's keys, have you?'

'Keys!' said Jennifer, and shook her hand in the air. In her hand was something small and shiny and rattly.

Jeremy James went a little closer.

'What have you got?' he asked.

Jennifer smiled.

'Show me,' said Jeremy James.

Jennifer smiled again and waddled to the other side of the playpen.

'Have you got Daddy's keys?' asked Jeremy James.

'Keys!' said Jennifer.

Jeremy James marched to the other side of the playpen.

Jennifer smiled.

'Jem Jem!' she said, and threw the small, shiny, rattly something out on to the carpet. Jeremy James picked it up. It was two keys and a leather tag on a ring.

'You *are* a naughty girl!' said Jeremy James, and raced at full throttle into Daddy's study.

'Are these the keys?' he asked.

Daddy's mouth flapped open like a car bonnet.

'Where were they?' he asked.

'In the living room,' said Jeremy James.

'They couldn't have been!' said Daddy. 'I looked all over the living room!'

Jeremy James thought he'd better not mention Jennifer. She had certainly done the finding, but she had almost certainly done the losing, too.

'They were just by the playpen,' he said – which was true because Jennifer had thrown them there.

'Well done, Jeremy James,' said Daddy. 'I must have dropped them when I was helping Mummy.'

That might have been true as well. But after Daddy had finally left, and while Mummy was washing up the breakfast things, Jeremy James asked Jennifer where she had found the keys. Jennifer smiled sweetly, and said:

'Jeffer nor-ty girl.'

It had been a typical Monday morning.

CHAPTER TWO

Yellow and Purple

'Look at that hair,' said Mummy.

Jeremy James tilted his head back and switched his eyes right up under his eyebrows, but he still couldn't see his hair.

'It's far too long,' said Mummy. 'He'd better have it cut.'

Mummy always cut Jeremy James's hair, but now she thought it was time he had it done properly at the barber's.

'I'm going into town this morning,' said Daddy. 'I'll take him, and he can have it cut while I'm at the library.'

An hour later, when Daddy had found his papers, pens, and the list of things he wanted to look up in the library, the two of them set off for town. Daddy took Jeremy James straight to the barber's, where he told a fat man with a moustache that he would come back for his son in an hour. The fat man nodded, and Jeremy James sat down in a chair against the wall to wait his turn.

'I shan't be long,' said Daddy, 'so just wait till I get back.'

There were two big chairs on the other side of the room in front of mirrors, and two men were sitting in the chairs having their hair cut. The fat man with a moustache was seeing to one, and a thin, pale young man was seeing to the other. Jeremy James could see the customers' faces in the mirrors. One of them (the fat man's) had had nearly all his hair cut off, and the fat man had just taken a razor to do the rest. The other one had the strangest hair Jeremy James had ever seen – it was yellow and purple, and some of it was standing up as stiff and straight as a brush.

A worried expression crossed Jeremy James's face. He didn't want *all* his hair cut off, so he hoped that the fat man wouldn't see to him. On the other hand, he didn't want yellow and purple hair either.

Jeremy James glanced at the man waiting in the chair next to him. He was an old man with a bald head and glasses, and he smiled at Jeremy James. Jeremy James didn't smile back. The worried look on his face was now joined by a puzzled look.

'Excuse me,' he said.

'What is it, sonny?' asked the old man kindly.

'If you've had your hair cut off,' said Jeremy James, 'why are you waiting?'

'I haven't had it cut off,' said the old man. 'And do you know why?'

'Why?' asked Jeremy James.

'Because,' said the old man, 'you can't cut off what isn't there. I lost my hair a long time ago.'

'Couldn't you find it again?' asked Jeremy James.

'I'm afraid not,' said the old man.

'I carry mine around with me,' said Jeremy James. 'On my head.'

'That's the best place to keep it,' said the old man.

Then Jeremy James again asked the old man why he was waiting, and the old man said he'd come for a shave, to get rid of the bristles on his chin.

'So you'll go to the fat man,' said Jeremy James. 'He's got the razor.'

'I expect Mr Simon will see to me, yes,' said the old man.

If the old man was going to the fat man, it meant that Jeremy James would not have all his hair cut off. That was good. But then Jeremy James would be going to the thin man, and that meant he would have yellow and purple hair. And that wasn't so good. Jeremy James began to wish that Daddy hadn't gone away.

The fat man finished balding his customer, who looked at himself in the mirror.

'Is that all right, sir?' asked the fat man.

'Yeah, OK, 's fine, OK, yeah,' said the newly bald man.

He gave the fat man some money, and Jeremy James watched as the shiny head went past him like a walking lollipop, and left the shop.

The old man next to Jeremy James got up from his chair.

'Hallo, Mr Williams,' said the fat man.

'Hallo, Frederick,' said the old man. 'It seems I've started a fashion, eh?'

They both laughed, though Jeremy James couldn't

see what there was to laugh at. On the contrary, he felt more like crying than laughing. No hair in one chair, and coloured spikes in the other – it was no laughing matter at all. Maybe Daddy didn't know what they did at this barber's. Mummy often said that Daddy lived in a world of his own, so how *could* he know? If only he would come back quickly, before it was Jeremy James's turn to sit in the chair.

But Daddy didn't come back. And the yellow-and-purple man was looking at himself in the mirror.

'Very nice,' he said.

'Is it to sir's satisfaction?' asked the thin pale man.

'Yeah, very nice,' said Yellow-and-Purple. 'I like it. It's very nice. Very nice. That's what it is. Yeah.'

He gave the thin pale man some money, and Jeremy James watched as the bristly head went past him, like a walking toothbrush.

'Your turn now, son,' said the thin pale man to Jeremy James.

Jeremy James turned as pale as the thin pale man. He stood up. Yellow-and-Purple had just opened the shop door. Jeremy James looked at the door, looked at the thin pale man, looked at the chair, and then ran as fast as he could straight past Yellow-and-Purple and out into the street.

'Come back!' shouted a voice.

Jeremy James had no intention of going back, but when he glanced behind him, he saw that the thin pale man and the yellow-and-purple man were both running after him.

'Stop him!' they shouted.

Jeremy James looked to the front again, and found himself running straight into a pair of dark blue trousers.

'Oops!' said a deep voice.

'Ouf!' said Jeremy James.

Then he was lifted high into the air until he was face to face with a silver badge on a helmet.

'Now where are you off to in such a 'urry, me lad?' asked the policeman.

With a phew and a puff and a gasp the thin pale man and Yellow-and-Purple came up to the policeman.

'No!' shouted Jeremy James. 'Go away! Go away!'

The policeman joggled him up and down in his arms.

'You're all right, sonny,' he said. 'You're quite safe wi' me. Now I wants to know what's goin' on.'

The thin pale man told the policeman that the little boy's father had left him to have his hair cut, but he had run out of the shop.

'Is that right?' asked the policeman.

Jeremy James pointed to the yellow and purple spikes.

'I don't want them . . .' he sobbed. 'I don't want to be yellow and purple.'

'I'm not surprised,' said the policeman. 'Nor would I. But you won't be like that. Did you think you were going to be like that?'

'Yes,' said Jeremy James.

The policeman laughed out loud, and the other two men laughed as well. But Jeremy James knew it wasn't funny, because if his hair was not to be yellow and purple, it was to be cut off, and that was just as bad.

'I don't . . . I don't . . .' he sobbed, 'I don't want to be balded either.'

'Balded?' said the policeman.

'By the fat man,' said Jeremy James.

'I think,' said the policeman, 'that this case is a bit more serious than we'd thought. What's yer name, son?'

'Jeremy James,' said Jeremy James.

'Right, Jeremy James,' said the policeman. 'We'd better let your Dad sort it out. Where is he?'

Jeremy James told the policeman that Daddy was in the library, and so he and the policeman walked hand in hand up the street, left at the traffic lights, across the zebra crossing, round the corner, and into the library.

Daddy was very surprised to see a policeman come into the library with Jeremy James. He was so surprised that he dropped his pen, made a grab for it, and in so doing knocked a thick book off the table and on to the floor. Several people turned round and said, 'Sh!'

The policeman and Daddy and Jeremy James all went outside so that the policeman could explain what had happened.

'If I was you, sir,' said the policeman, 'I wouldn't leave a little lad alone in a strange place. You never know what little lads can start thinking.'

Daddy thanked the policeman, who said goodbye to Jeremy James and walked away, shaking his head.

'You know what I think we should do, Jeremy James?' said Daddy. 'I think we should go home and let Mummy cut your hair as usual. Don't you?'

Jeremy James did.

CHAPTER THREE

A Note in the Wind

Jeremy James had gone to Richard's house to play. Round and red-faced Richard lived at No. 24, with his round and red-faced mother, his thin and pale-faced father, and his tiny wrinkled grandmother. Jeremy James liked them all except Gran, who had a funny smell and a loud voice. Richard's mother had once told Jeremy James that Gran was a little deaf. Richard said he wished he was deaf sometimes so that he couldn't hear Gran's loud voice.

It was a windy day, and the boys were in the garden playing with Richard's model glider. They threw it high in the air, and watched it swoop and swerve in the wind until it either levelled out into a perfect landing, or – more frequently – nose-dived straight into the grass. It was great fun, and they were really enjoying themselves when . . .

'Richard!'

'Oh no,' said Richard, 'it's Gran.'

'Richard!'

'I'm coming, Gran!'

'Richard!'

'I'll have to go and see what she wants,' said Richard.

Gran wanted some cigarettes. She gave Richard five pounds and said he could buy some sweets for himself and Jeremy James.

'She's quite nice really,' said Richard. 'It's just that she doesn't *seem* nice.'

Gran had also given him a letter addressed to the shop man (because otherwise he wouldn't let Richard have the cigarettes), and so Richard put the letter in one pocket, the five-pound note in the other, and set off with Jeremy James.

'I don't know why she smokes cigarettes, anyway,' said Richard. 'She's always coughing.'

'I expect that's what made her go deaf,' said Jeremy James.

'Yes, so she wouldn't hear herself coughing,' said Richard.

'And she's got a funny smell, your Gran,' said Jeremy James. 'She ought to stop smoking.'

'She does,' said Richard. 'But then she starts again.'

The playground was on the way to the shop, and so Richard and Jeremy James went for a swing and a see-saw. Then they slid on the slide and rode on the roundabout. And after that they went to the shop. When they got to the shop, Richard pulled the letter out of one pocket, felt in the other and . . .

'It's gone!' cried Richard.

'What's gone?' asked Mr Drew, the shop man.

'The five pounds!' cried Richard. 'The five pounds has gone!'

Mr Drew had grey hair, twinkling grey eyes, and a kind heart.

'Steady on, lad,' he said. 'Don't panic. Have a good look through your pockets.'

But apart from a piece of string, a rubber band, a toffee-wrapper, a paper handkerchief, an old bus ticket, a blob of fluff, a feather, half a pencil and another piece of string, Richard's pockets were empty.

'What about you, Jeremy James?' asked Mr Drew. 'You sure you haven't got it?'

Jeremy James hadn't got it either.

'Well I'll tell you what to do,' said Mr Drew. 'Go back over everywhere you've been, and search carefully. It can't have gone far. I'd come with you, only I can't leave the shop, you see.'

Richard and Jeremy James went back down the street, with their noses almost scraping the pavement as they searched. Richard couldn't see very much, though, because his eyes were filled with tears.

'Gran'll kill me!' he sobbed. 'I'm not going home. I'm going to run away.'

'Maybe it's in the playground,' said Jeremy James.

Like two bloodhounds they shuffled, heads down, between the swing and the see-saw, the slide and the roundabout – but there was no five-pound note.

'It's blown away!' cried Richard. 'We'll never see it again!'

A man came by with a dog.

'Excuse me,' said Jeremy James. 'You haven't seen a five-pound note, have you?'

'I do occasionally see them,' said the man. 'Any particular one?'

'Richard's,' said Jeremy James. 'It's a blue one.'

'Ah!' said the man. 'Lost it, has he?'

'Yes,' said Jeremy James.

But the man hadn't seen it. And his dog hadn't seen it either. And a lady who came by pushing a pram hadn't seen it, and another lady with a shopping basket hadn't seen it, and the park attendant with the peaked cap and the red nose hadn't seen it. They all had a look round, but they all thought the wind must have taken it.

'And if the wind ain't took it,' said the park attendant, 'then someone else 'as!'

'I'm never going home!' sobbed Richard. 'I'll run away to sea.'

'To see what?' asked Jeremy James.

'To sea,' said Richard. 'On a boat. Like Grandad.'

'Does your grandad live on a boat?' asked Jeremy James.

'No, he doesn't live anywhere now,' said Richard. 'He's dead. But he lived on a boat when he was alive.'

'I expect he wanted to get away from Gran,' said Jeremy James.

Since Richard couldn't go home, and since he didn't want to run away to sea just yet, Jeremy James suggested he should come and live at Jeremy James's house.

'Do you think your mummy'll mind?' asked Richard.

'No,' said Jeremy James. 'She likes children.'

And so the two boys went to Jeremy James's house.

'Oh, hello,' said Mummy, 'I thought you were both playing at Richard's house today.'

'No,' said Jeremy James, 'Richard's run away, so he's coming to live with us. Is that all right, Mummy?'

'Oh!' said Mummy. 'Well, it would be nice to have Richard living with us, but I don't think *his* mummy'll be very pleased. Have you told her, Richard?'

'Well, no . . . not yet,' said Richard. 'But I don't think she'll mind.'

Then Mummy asked Richard why he'd run away. Richard started explaining what had happened, and Jeremy James finished explaining what had happened, because Richard began to cry again.

'I see,' said Mummy, and sat there thinking for a minute or two. Then she looked at Richard, who was still crying, and she looked at Jeremy James, who was looking at Richard crying, and she said:

'Now that's very strange. That's very strange indeed. Just wait a moment.'

She went to her handbag, opened it, and felt inside. Then she pulled out a five-pound note.

'Was it a blue one like this?'

Richard stopped crying, and both boys peered closely at the five-pound note.

'Yes, it was,' said Jeremy James.

'And did it have numbers on it like these?' asked Mummy.

'Yes, I think so,' said Richard.

'And did it have a picture of the Queen like this?' asked Mummy.

'I think so,' said Richard.

'Well that *is* a stroke of luck,' said Mummy. 'Because when I opened the front door just now, the wind blew this five-pound note straight into my hand. So it must be yours, Richard. Now I think you'd better hurry back to the shop for Gran's cigarettes, or she'll wonder where you've got to.'

Richard and Jeremy James ran all the way back to the shop.

'Ah, you found it then!' said Mr Drew.

Jeremy James explained how the wind had blown the five-pound note into Mummy's hand, and Mr Drew's eyes twinkled even more merrily than usual.

'Fancy that!' he said. 'Now I'll tell *you* something. I was sweeping the floor just now, and under the counter I found two pound coins and a 50p piece. And I happen to know, Jeremy James, that they all belong to your mother, who must have dropped them when she came in yesterday. Would you give them to her, please, and tell her they're from me.'

Jeremy James took the three coins, and Richard bought the cigarettes and sweets and put the change carefully in his pocket.

'Make sure you don't lose it,' said Mr Drew.

'I won't,' said Richard and Jeremy James together.

When the two boys got back to Richard's house,

Gran was fast asleep, so she couldn't have noticed how long they'd been.

'She's always asleep,' said Richard.

'I expect the smoke gets in her eyes,' said Jeremy James.

At teatime, Jeremy James went home and gave the money to Mummy. She was quite surprised to get it, but when Jeremy James told her what Mr Drew had said, she nodded and smiled.

'We all seem to be losing our money,' she said.

'*And* finding it,' said Jeremy James.

'That's right,' said Mummy. 'We *are* lucky.'

And her eyes were twinkling just like Mr Drew's.

CHAPTER FOUR

A Present from Timothy

'No, I don't want to invite *him*,' said Jeremy James. 'He always spoils everything.'

'I know,' said Mummy, 'but we don't want to offend the Smyth-Fortescues.'

Him was Timothy, who lived next door, was a year older than Jeremy James, and knew everything about everything.

'I don't mind offending the Smile-Fortyqueues,' said Jeremy James.

'You'll have to invite him all the same,' said Mummy.

The invitation was to Jeremy James's birthday party, and inviting Timothy would be like asking an elephant to share your glass of lemonade. What was shared with Timothy became Timothy's.

'Go round and tell him now,' said Mummy.

'Do I have to?' moaned Jeremy James, trying to disappear into the floor.

'Yes,' said Mummy.

Mrs Smyth-Fortescue opened the door when Jeremy James rang to deliver the invitation.

'Oh, how lovely!' she said. 'He loves parties.'

'But if he's doing something else,' said Jeremy James, 'I'll be very pleased.'

'No, of course he isn't. Are you, dear?'

'No,' said Timothy. 'I don't mind coming to your party, though it won't be as good as mine.'

'Thank you so much, Jeremy,' said Mrs Smyth-Fortescue, who never remembered to call him Jeremy James. 'Timothy will be there, don't worry.'

It was because Timothy would be there that Jeremy James did worry, but at least it would mean an extra present.

'Don't forget my present,' he said to Timothy.

'Your presents won't be as good as mine,' said Timothy.

The birthday began with a red pedal-car from Mummy and Daddy, which had a horn that really hooted and lights that really lit. Jeremy James spent most of the morning in his pedal-car, but as it was raining outside, he couldn't give it a proper speed-test. Instead he tested the steering – round and some-times into the furniture – the lights, and especially the horn. For some reason Daddy told Mummy the horn had been a mistake, but Jeremy James couldn't find anything wrong with it.

Other presents included a football from the twins, and a big box of games from Uncle Jack, Aunt Janet and cousin Melissa. These were morning presents from the family. Next there would be afternoon presents from the friends.

One by one they arrived. Little Trevor came with a bag of sweets (he'd tried them and said they were

very nice), fat Richard brought a model glider, and
there were books and toys and games which Jeremy
James laid out on the sideboard so that everyone
could see what he'd got.

But the most interesting present was Timothy's.
At first Timothy wouldn't even give it to him.

'You're too young,' he said. 'My mummy really
bought it for me, and I don't think you should have it.'

'Then why's it wrapped in birthday paper?' asked
Jeremy James.

Mummy came by at that moment, and noticed
that not only was it wrapped in birthday paper, but
it also had Jeremy James's name on it.

Timothy pulled a grumpy face, and thrust out the
packet without even looking at Jeremy James.

'There you are,' he said. 'But it's not really for little kids like you.'

Jeremy James opened the packet. Inside the wrapping paper was a white box which was small, but quite heavy. Jeremy James opened the white box, and found something that looked like a pocket-knife but wasn't.

'It's a torch,' said Timothy, 'and it's got a compass and a magnifying glass and a screwdriver and a bottle-opener and a ruler and . . . well, it's really for me. I should have had it, not you.'

Jeremy James loved the torch. It was his second-best present after the pedal-car, and he put it right at the front of his pile of things on the sideboard. The other children liked it, too, and when they'd had a sit in the pedal-car and had flashed the lights and honked the horn, most of them wanted to look through the magnifying glass, switch the torch on and off, and turn the compass around. Timothy stayed beside it to show everyone how it worked, and to make sure they knew it came from him. He wasn't interested in the pedal-car anyway, because he had a bigger one with a horn and lights and a lift-up bonnet and a slide-over roof.

The party was a great success. The crisps and crackers, buns and biscuits, jam tarts and jellies all disappeared without leaving a trace, and nobody was sick. There were no tears in any of the games, and everybody won a prize. Timothy didn't cheat, and didn't even tell Jeremy James that his own party had been better. In fact, Timothy hardly said a word all afternoon, which was as strange as a monkey not eating bananas.

When at last it was time for everyone to leave, Mummy gave them all a packet of sweets and a little game to take home with them. Then, as the first goodbyes were being said, Jeremy James saw something. To be more precise, Jeremy James didn't see something. What he didn't see was his torch-compass-magnifying glass.

'Where's my torch?' he cried.

Mummy came to have a look. Then Daddy came to have a look. And then all the children came to have a look. And what they all looked at was the space where the torch had been and now was not.

'It's gone,' said Daddy.

'Maybe it's fallen behind the sideboard,' said Mummy.

But it hadn't.

'Maybe it's fallen into Timothy's pocket,' said Jeremy James.

'Yes,' said fat Richard, 'I bet Timothy's got it.'

'No I haven't!' said Timothy, going as red as a jam tart. 'I haven't got it! I haven't!'

'Of course you haven't,' said Mummy quickly. 'You mustn't say things like that, Jeremy James.'

'I bet he has, though,' said Jeremy James to Richard.

Mummy now called the children together and told them they were going to play one last game.

'I want you to stand round the sideboard,' she said, 'and when I tell you to, close your eyes and wish very hard that the torch comes back. Will you do that?'

'Yes!' said a dozen voices.

Mummy placed the children in front of the side-board, and she got Timothy to stand right by the spot where the torch had been.

'Now if the torch doesn't come back,' said Mummy, 'we'll all empty our pockets, just in case the torch accidentally fell into one. Right?'

'Yes!' said a dozen voices.

'Good,' said Mummy. 'Now then, close your eyes and don't open them till I tell you to. Otherwise you'll break the magic spell. And if anyone *does* open his eyes, he'll lose his prizes and his sweets and his present.'

A dozen pairs of eyes were tightly closed.

'Now wish with all your might that the torch comes back.'

There was a rich and wishy silence as a dozen children (minus one) willed the torch back on to the sideboard. Jeremy James thought he heard a move-ment next to him. He opened his eyes to tiny slits, and saw Timothy stepping back from the sideboard.

'You can open your eyes now,' said Mummy.

The eyes opened. Then the mouths opened as well, for there on the sideboard was the torch.

'Well done, everybody,' said Mummy.

'Sheer magic!' said Daddy.

'Timothy moved,' said Jeremy James.

'No, I didn't,' said Timothy.

'Did anybody see Timothy move?' asked Mummy.

Jeremy James did some quick thinking. He *had* seen Timothy move, but in order to see him, he'd had to open his eyes, and Mummy had said that anyone opening his eyes would lose prizes, sweets and present. Or had she perhaps even said presents? Jeremy James kept quiet. So did fat Richard and little Trevor.

'Mummy,' said Jeremy James, when everyone had gone home. 'Timothy did move.'

'Yes, I know,' said Mummy.

'Then he should have lost his prizes and sweets,' said Jeremy James.

'But you,' said Mummy, 'opened your eyes, didn't you?'

'Um . . . yes,' said Jeremy James.

'So you,' said Mummy, 'should have lost your prizes and sweets *and* presents.'

'Hmmph,' said Jeremy James, and went to look at his car through the magnifying glass.

CHAPTER FIVE

A Frightening Experience

Daddy and Jeremy James were going fishing. Fishing was Daddy's latest hobby, and he said it was much more enjoyable than football, television, and paying bills. As Jeremy James had never been fishing, Mummy suggested he should go with Daddy, and as Jeremy James was not doing anything special that afternoon, he and Daddy duly set off for the river. Daddy was carrying a big bag and had his fishing rod slung over his shoulder like a nervous rifle. Over Jeremy James's shoulder was a net, and he was carrying a tin that was full of squiggly maggots.

'What are the maggots for?' asked Jeremy James.

'Bait,' said Daddy.

'What's bait?' asked Jeremy James.

'We put the maggot on the hook,' said Daddy, 'then the fish tries to eat the maggot and gets caught on the hook.'

Jeremy James thought Daddy should put chocolate or liquorice allsorts on the hook, but Daddy said fish preferred maggots.

Jeremy James thought fish must be very silly creatures, and he felt sorry for the maggots.

'This looks a good spot,' said Daddy, when they had reached the river. 'Let's try here.'

He took two folding stools out of the bag and set them on the ground. Then he took a maggot out of the tin and fixed it on the hook of his fishing line.

'Doesn't that hurt?' asked Jeremy James.

'Ouch!' said Daddy, sticking the hook in his thumb. 'Yes, it does!'

'I meant the maggot,' said Jeremy James.

Daddy told Jeremy James to stand clear, and with a swing and a heave he threw the maggot, hook and line far out into the water where they landed with a plop, and disappeared from view.

'Now,' said Daddy, 'you see the red-and-white float bobbing up and down?'

'Yes,' said Jeremy James.

'Well, if it moves around, we've got a bite, and if it goes under the water, we've got a fish. So watch carefully.'

They both sat down on the folding stools and watched the red-and-white float. It bobbed gently up and down, but it didn't move around and it didn't go under the water.

'How long will it be?' asked Jeremy James.

'I don't know,' said Daddy. 'Fish are a bit like trains – you never know how long they'll keep you waiting.'

Daddy and Jeremy James waited a long time. But the red-and-white float still didn't move around and still didn't go under the water.

'Maybe the maggot's run away,' said Jeremy James.

'Or gone for a swim,' said Daddy.

He wound the line in, and the float came up out of the water, followed by an empty, maggotless hook.

Three times Daddy threw hooked maggots into the water, three times they waited and watched, and three times the hook came back empty.

'Can't even catch a maggot!' grumbled Daddy.

Jeremy James had decided that fishing was the silliest, boringest, pointlessest game he'd ever played when suddenly . . .

'We've got a bite!' said Daddy.

Jeremy James fixed his eyes on the red-and-white float, and sure enough it was ducking and jerking in all directions. A moment later, under it went.

'Got you!' said Daddy, and began to wind in the line. 'Quite a big one, too, from the way it's pulling.'

Jeremy James watched as the float came up out of the water.

'Now get the net ready, Jeremy James,' said Daddy, 'and as soon as the fish comes near, see if you can catch it in the net.'

Out came the fish. It *was* a big one, and it was flashing silver in the sun as it writhed and wriggled on the hook. Nearer and nearer it came, and Jeremy James reached out the net to catch it. And that was the moment when a terrible thing happened. Jeremy James reached out too far, his foot slipped on a patch of mud, and as the fish came from water to bank, so Jeremy James went from bank to water. There was a loud splash as he tumbled head first into a cold, swirling wetness that closed over his head with a loud gurgling roar.

The water bellowed into his ears and blocked his nose and blurred his eyes. He kicked his legs and flailed his arms, trying to keep it away.

Suddenly his head was above the water, and he just had time to see the green bank and the trees and fields before once more he was sucked down, and the roaring filled his head again. He couldn't breathe. There was blackness all around him. He kicked and flailed.

Up he rose above the water. He gasped for air, crying as the air came into him. 'Daddy!' he shouted. But then his mouth filled with water again as the river pulled him down. He just saw a shape moving towards him before he went under, falling into rushing darkness, flashing lights, and a coldness that now made him too numb and weak even to kick. He was falling, falling, and the darkness was rising to meet him . . .

Something gripped his heavy body, and he was thrust up through the water like a rocket through the sky. Air. He gulped and cried and gulped and cried.

'You're all right, son,' said Daddy. 'You're all right.'

Daddy was in the water beside him, holding him up and wedging him so that he couldn't go down again. 'You're all right.'

Slowly and gently Daddy moved himself and Jeremy James through the water and across to the bank. Jeremy James was coughing and spluttering like Daddy's car on a winter's day.

'I'll just lift you up on to the bank,' said Daddy, 'and then you must pull yourself to the top. All right?'

Daddy lifted him high on to the bank, and he gripped the grass tightly. Then he felt Daddy's hand on his bottom, pushing him upwards, and he crawled to the top and lay on his stomach.

He suddenly felt very cold, and his teeth began to chatter. He couldn't stop crying. Somehow the tears kept coming out like a bubbling fountain, joining the river water that flowed down from his hair, his ears and his mouth.

'Come on, Jeremy James,' said Daddy. 'I think that's enough fishing for today. Let's go home.' He lifted Jeremy James on to his shoulder. But the fishing hadn't quite finished. As Daddy picked up the fishing rod, there was an unmistakable pull on the line (which had fallen back into the water).

'Well I'm blowed,' said Daddy.

Jeremy James looked round to see what was blowing Daddy, and he saw a big silver fish flying slowly through the air towards him.

'Nice of him to wait for us, wasn't it?' said Daddy.

When Mummy heard what had happened, she shook her head from side to side like a fish shaking its tail.

'It was all my fault,' said Daddy. 'I was watching the fish instead of Jeremy James.'

Daddy and Jeremy James dripped upstairs, and took off all their wet clothes. Then Jeremy James sat down in the nicest hot bath anyone had ever had.

By the time they came downstairs, Jeremy James had stopped crying and shivering and tooth-chattering, and instead felt warm and fresh and clean. And when his nose took in a delicious smell coming from the kitchen, he suddenly realized that he was very, very hungry.

'What's for supper?' he asked Mummy.

'Guess,' said Mummy.

'Fish,' said Jeremy James.

'And whose fish?' asked Daddy.

'My fish,' said Jeremy James.

Of all the fish that Jeremy James had ever tasted, his fish proved to be the tastiest. Mummy and Daddy each had a piece as well, and they both said it was the best fish ever.

'Almost worth diving into the river for,' said Daddy.

All the same, Jeremy James decided he didn't want to go fishing again. Fishing, he thought, was very dangerous – and not just for maggots.

CHAPTER SIX

Do Goldfish Play the Violin?

The goldfish pond in Aunt Janet's garden must have been quite deep, because you couldn't see the bottom. What you could see was a sort of dark jungle down below, and lots of green leaves on the top with the goldfish swimming in between them. It was the gold-fish that Jeremy James liked watching, though he kept well back from the edge of the pond to make sure he didn't fall in. He was holding Jennifer's hand, as he certainly didn't want her to go fishing.

'Fish!' said Jennifer.

'Goldfish!' said Jeremy James.

'Go fish!' said Jennifer.

'No,' said Jeremy James. 'That's dangerous.'

The two families were in the garden. The grown-ups were sitting in deckchairs, and Melissa – who was the same age as Jeremy James – had just come out of the living room and was showing Christopher her new doll. Christopher was not interested in the new doll or in Melissa, and toddled hurriedly across the lawn to Mummy.

It was a happy, peaceful scene, with the sun shin-ing, birds singing, bees buzzing, and everybody quietly and contentedly occupied. Then Aunt Janet made an announcement.

'Now, my dears, we're going to have a special treat. Is everything ready, Melissa?'

'Yes, Mummy,' said Melissa.

'Right, I want you all to come into the living room. The children, too. Come along, Jeremy James and Jennifer.'

They all trooped into the living room, where Aunt Janet asked everyone to sit down. Then Melissa put a sheet of paper on a strange-looking metal what's-a-name.

'Melissa,' said Aunt Janet, 'is going to play the violin for us.'

Melissa opened a black box and took out her violin.

'She's only been learning for six months,' said Aunt Janet, 'but she's *so* gifted. Are you ready, Melissa? Good. She's going to play six pieces by Sir Edward Elgar. Shush, everybody! Right, Melissa, dear, we're all listening.'

Melissa stood with her pigtails at the back of her neck and her violin at the front, and pulled a sort of stringy stick across the violin. The sound that came out went through the room like a needle through a buttonhole. The only similar sound Jeremy James had ever heard was Christopher's raging screech when Jennifer snatched a toy from him. It was a high, piercing wail that shook your eardrums till your teeth rattled. Melissa's violin wail was not as loud as Christopher's, but it contained the same degree of pain.

Jeremy James stole a look at Mummy and Daddy. Mummy was sitting with a funny smile on her face, gazing straight at Melissa as if she were listening carefully. Daddy was also gazing at Melissa, but he had screwed up his eyes, which actually closed at one moment, and Jeremy James noticed that his mouth was shut tight, as if he was gritting his teeth.

Melissa stopped, and the grown-ups clapped while Aunt Janet cried, 'Well done, darling!'

The piece hadn't lasted long, and Jeremy James was about to get up when Aunt Janet spoke again: 'Now for the second piece.'

The second piece sounded exactly the same as the first, until Jeremy James thought there were two violins playing. The second violin, however, turned out to be Christopher, whose wail contained some notes that Sir Edward Elgar had never imagined.

Mummy glanced apologetically at Aunt Janet, and slipped out into the garden with Christopher. Jeremy James managed not to glance at Aunt Janet, and he also slipped out into the garden. The scraping shrillness followed, but it didn't hurt quite so much from further away.

There was another light shower of applause from the living room, then Aunt Janet appeared at the patio door.

'Are you coming back in?' she asked.

'We'd better not,' said Mummy. 'Our Christopher's not a great music-lover, I'm afraid. But we can hear quite well anyway.'

Aunt Janet went back into the living room.

'I'm not a great music-lover either,' said Jeremy James.

From inside the living room they heard Daddy say, 'No, no, carry on. It's really . . . ugh, ugh . . . lovely.'

Mummy, Jeremy James and Christopher wandered down to look at the goldfish. They watched the fish dart through the leaves as swiftly as Melissa's bow darted over the wrong strings, and it was then that Jeremy James had an idea.

When Melissa had finished playing (and heavily defeating) Sir Edward Elgar, Mummy went to change the twins' nappies, Uncle Jack took Daddy out to see his new car, and Aunt Janet went to the kitchen to prepare tea. That left Jeremy James and Melissa to play games together. Jeremy James hated playing games with Melissa, but today was going to be different.

'Let's play Freezing,' he said.

He had played Freezing with Melissa once before. One person had to hide something, and the other tried to find it. The hider told the seeker he was freezing, cold, warm, or hot according to how near the seeker was. Melissa had found Jeremy James's sweet wrapper in no time at all, but Jeremy James hadn't found his toy car, which Melissa had hidden in her doll's knickers.

'Right,' said Melissa. 'I'll do the hiding.'

She hid a pin in the pocket of her dress, so that she could keep moving around making Jeremy James cold. But that was the trick she had used with the car and the doll, and it wasn't long before Jeremy James found the pin.

'Now I'll hide something,' said Jeremy James. 'Go in the front room till I call *ready*.'

'I'm only counting up to one hundred,' said Melissa, 'then I'm coming whether you're ready or not.'

Jeremy James had to be quick, and he *was* quick. By the time Melissa had reached one hundred, he was back in the living room and had closed the patio door.

Melissa searched the living room, and she searched Jeremy James, but she was freezing wherever she went.

'You'll never find it,' said Jeremy James. 'I've won.'

'No you haven't,' said Melissa. 'I know where it is.'

'Where?' said Jeremy James.

'It's in the garden,' said Melissa.

She opened the patio door.

'Just a bit warmer,' said Jeremy James.

Melissa went out into the garden, and the further she went, the warmer she became.

'Very hot,' said Jeremy James at last. Melissa was standing on the edge of the goldfish pond.

'It's in the pond,' said Melissa.

'Right,' said Jeremy James.

'So I've won,' said Melissa.

'No you haven't,' said Jeremy James. 'Because you haven't found it yet.'

'Yes I have,' said Melissa. 'I've found it in the pond.

'What is it, then?' asked Jeremy James.

'I don't know,' said Melissa.

'Then I've won,' said Jeremy James.

'No you haven't!' said Melissa.

'Yes I have,' said Jeremy James.

'It's not fair!' said Melissa.

'Yes it is,' said Jeremy James.

Melissa started crying, and Aunt Janet came out to see what was the matter, followed by Mummy a moment later. Melissa said Jeremy James had cheated, and Jeremy James said he hadn't, and Melissa's crying turned into a howling that reminded Jeremy James of Sir Woodhead Elgar.

Not even Uncle Jack or Daddy quite knew the rules of Freezing, and so no one could really say whether Jeremy James had cheated or not. The grown-ups therefore suggested the game should be called a draw, but Melissa said she'd won, and stamped off to her bedroom and slammed the door behind her.

'Oh dear!' said Aunt Janet. 'They do take these games so seriously, don't they?'

It was not until a couple of hours later, when Mummy, Daddy, the twins and Jeremy James were driving home, that an interesting question occurred to Daddy.

'Jeremy James,' he said, 'in that game of Freezing, what exactly *did* you throw in the goldfish pond?'

'The black box,' said Jeremy James.

'What black box?' asked Daddy.

'The black box with Melissa's violin,' said Jeremy James.

Daddy just managed to stop the car from swerving off the road, and Mummy let out a gasp that sounded just like one of Melissa's wrong notes.

As soon as they got home, Mummy telephoned Aunt Janet, while Daddy explained to Jeremy James that violins were very expensive, and throwing a violin into a goldfish pond could ruin it, as well as ruining the father who would have to pay for it.

'It was very naughty of you,' said Daddy, 'and you must never do such a thing again.'

'No, Daddy,' said Jeremy James.

'Though just between ourselves,' said Daddy, 'I'd sooner hear the goldfish play it than your cousin Melissa.'

Daddy wasn't a great music-lover either.

CHAPTER SEVEN

The Battleaxe

There was a very important lady coming to tea.

'Is it the Queen?' asked Jeremy James.

'Well, no,' said Daddy, 'she's not *that* important.'

'It's a lady who runs a theatre,' said Mummy, 'and that's very important for Daddy. So we must all be on our best behaviour. What's she like anyway, John?'

'A battleaxe,' said Daddy.

'What is a battleaxe?' asked Jeremy James.

'You'll see,' said Daddy.

'I hope she likes strawberries and cream,' said Mummy.

'*I* do,' said Jeremy James.

'I know you do,' said Mummy, 'but I've met you before, haven't I?'

Mummy prepared the things for tea, Daddy looked for things to show the lady, the twins played quietly, then loudly – Christopher hurt his finger – in their playpen, and Jeremy James looked out of his bedroom window, watching for the very important lady. It was a pity she wasn't as important as the Queen, but she was important enough for strawberries and cream, and if she was a sort of axe as well, she was worth watching for.

A big black car drew up outside the house, and Jeremy James rushed downstairs to Daddy's study.

'There's a big black car, Daddy!' he cried. 'It's the very important lady!'

The doorbell rang, and Daddy went into the hall, with Jeremy James right behind him.

'Hello, John,' said a deep voice.

'Hello, Lilian,' said Daddy. 'Lovely to see you. Come in.'

And in stepped . . . well, was it a man or a woman? Wide-eyed, Jeremy James peeped round Daddy at a pair of grey trousers, a grey jacket, a collar and tie, and a rather lined face under a bush of grey hair.

'Hello,' said the lady to Jeremy James.

Jeremy James's lips said, 'Hello,' but his voice stayed behind and said nothing.

'This is Jeremy James,' said Daddy.

'Pleased to meet you, Jeremy James,' said the lady, and bent down to shake his hand. Jeremy James's arm flapped as limply as a broken wing, and his mouth gaped as if he were waiting to be fed.

Mummy came from the kitchen into the hall.

'This is my wife,' said Daddy. 'Darling, this is Lilian da Costa.'

There were more handshakes and pleased-to-meet-you's, and then the lady was introduced to the twins. Jennifer immediately pulled herself to her feet and smiled sweetly, but Christopher withdrew into the far corner of the playpen and looked very, very serious.

'Lovely children!' boomed the lady. 'You must be very proud of them.'

Christopher's serious face crumpled into tragedy. 'Wah!' he howled. 'Wah! Wah!'

'Oh dear,' said Mummy. 'He's a bit shy of strangers.'

Jeremy James was not surprised. There couldn't be many strangers that were stranger than this one.

Daddy took the lady into his study so that they could talk quietly, and when Mummy had calmed Christopher down, she and Jeremy James went into the kitchen together.

'Mummy,' said Jeremy James, 'is she a man?'

'Sh!' whispered Mummy. 'Not so loud! No, she's a woman.'

'But she looks like a man!' whispered Jeremy James.

'I know,' said Mummy, 'but you don't get men called Lilian. Now off you go to your room, and I'll call you when it's teatime.'

Jeremy James wandered upstairs. From Daddy's study came the sound of a deep voice that wasn't Daddy's. If a woman looked like a man and sounded like a man, why wasn't she a man? Perhaps, thought Jeremy James, that was what was meant by a battleaxe.

Jeremy James could hardly wait for tea, but not because of the strawberries. He wanted to see the important lady again. And he wanted to ask her some questions. So when Mummy at last called out, 'Jeremy James, it's time for . . .' he was already at the table in time for 'tea'.

Daddy and the lady were sitting there, and the lady was looking serious and saying: 'If the d— government keep slapping their d— taxes on theatre tickets, we shall all d— well be out of business!'

Jeremy James wondered if Mummy would tell the lady off for saying naughty words, but Mummy was pouring tea and didn't seem to have heard.

Jeremy James sat in his usual chair and looked at the lady.

Then the lady looked at Jeremy James.

'Now then, young man,' she said, 'what have you got to say for yourself?'

'Well,' said Jeremy James, 'are you *really* a woman?'

'Jeremy James!' exclaimed Mummy, pouring milk on to the tablecloth.

'That's all right, my dear,' said the lady. 'Yes, Jeremy James, I am *really* a woman.'

'Then why have you got such a deep voice?' asked Jeremy James.

'Are you a man?' asked the lady.

'Well, nearly,' said Jeremy James.

'Then why have you got such a high voice?' asked the lady.

Jeremy James didn't know, but he thought his voice would get deeper when he grew older. Then the lady said that was exactly what had happened to *her* voice.

'And there's nothing,' said the lady, 'that you or I can do about it.'

'Well why do you wear men's clothes?' asked Jeremy James.

Daddy had a little fit of coughing, and Mummy waved her hands in the air and said Jeremy James had asked enough questions, but the lady smiled and said:

'I wear 'em because I like 'em. Would you like to wear a dress, Jeremy James?'

'No thank you,' said Jeremy James.

'Nor would I,' said the lady. 'So I don't. And nor do you.'

'Do have some more scones,' said Mummy, 'and Jeremy James, let's have less talk. Just get on with your tea.'

Mummy gave Jeremy James a buttered scone with jam on it, and at the same time asked the lady a question about her theatre. Jeremy James munched and listened wonderingly to the deep voice, while Mummy and Daddy nodded and occasionally murmured 'yes' or 'mhm' or 'of course'.

After the scones came the long-awaited strawberries and cream, so Jeremy James was far too busy to ask any questions. But when he'd finished (and the lady had only just *started* her strawberries), there was a sudden silence at the table, so that he was able to ask the question he'd been wanting to ask all afternoon.

'What *is* a battleaxe?'

The silence after this question was even more

silent than the silence before. Eventually Mummy, whose face had gone a little white, said to no one in particular:

'I just don't know where he gets these words from!'

'From Daddy,' said Jeremy James.

'Ugh!' said Daddy.

Suddenly there was a most extraordinary noise. It was like elephant trumpet-calls with frog-croaks in between, and the calls and the croaks were all coming from the lady. She was laughing. And as she laughed, her shoulders shook and her head waggled up and down like a pecking bird. Jeremy James had never seen anyone laugh like that. It was a laugh that made you laugh just to hear it, and before long Jeremy James was laughing, Mummy and Daddy were laughing, and even Jennifer in the playpen was laughing. Only Christopher, on the other side of the playpen, had failed to notice anything funny.

It was a long time before the laughter died down, but at last the lady wiped her eyes, said, 'Oh dear!' several times, gave a couple more trumpet hoots, and then shook her head from side to side.

'So you want to know . . . toot . . . what a battle-axe is,' she said. 'Well, Jeremy James, a battleaxe is a strong and bossy woman who gets what she wants because she's strong and bossy. I am a battleaxe.'

'No, really . . .' said Daddy.

'Do you always get what you want?' asked Jeremy James.

'Always,' said the lady. 'Shall I prove it?'

'Yes,' said Jeremy James.

'Right,' said the lady. 'I want you to have some more strawberries.'

Jeremy James looked at the lady, and the lady looked at Jeremy James, and they both started smiling again. Then Jeremy James looked at Mummy, Mummy looked at the lady, the lady looked at Mummy, and Mummy looked at Jeremy James. Mummy put some more strawberries in Jeremy James's bowl.

'Now I want you to eat 'em,' said the lady.

Thus the lady proved that she always got what she wanted. And when Mummy asked her if *she* would like some more strawberries, she also proved that she got what she liked.

The rest of tea was very jolly and everyone laughed a lot, especially when the lady laughed. Jeremy James was really sorry when at last she said it was time for her to leave.

'I want you to stay,' he said.

'If you were a battleaxe,' said the lady, 'I'd have to, but you're not, and I can't.'

She kissed Mummy and Daddy goodbye, and asked if she could have a kiss from Jeremy James. He gave her a very big warm smacky one.

'I haven't laughed so much in years,' she said to Daddy. 'You ought to put your family on the stage to cheer everyone up.'

Jeremy James waved until the big black car had disappeared, and then asked Mummy what had made the lady laugh so much. Mummy explained that

Daddy's calling her a battleaxe had been a sort of secret, because 'battleaxe' was a rather rude word.

'Some people would have been angry,' said Mummy, 'but Mrs da Costa thought it was funny. Fortunately.'

Jeremy James didn't see why anyone should be angry.

'I think,' said Jeremy James, 'that battleaxes are nice. And I wish I was one.'

CHAPTER EIGHT

How to Stop Paying Bills

It was Jeremy James's job to fetch the post in the morning. Most of it was for Daddy, and came in printed brown envelopes which made Daddy say, 'Ugh!' Mummy's letters were usually hand-written, and Jeremy James only had post at Christmas time and on his birthday. He would have liked more letters, and he would also have liked more Christmases and more birthdays.

On this particular morning, there had only been one letter – a printed brown envelope for Daddy.

'Ugh!' said Daddy. 'Another bill.'

He opened the brown envelope, took out a printed piece of paper, unfolded it, and said, 'Oh!'

'How much?' asked Mummy.

'Seventy-two pounds,' said Daddy.

Then Mummy said, 'Oh!' as well.

'What exactly *are* bills?' asked Jeremy James.

'A worple worple nuisance,' said Daddy.

'Bills,' said Mummy, 'are what you pay for things like gas, water, electricity, the phone. Whatever you use has to be paid for, and you know how much to pay when you get the bill.'

For the rest of the day, when he wasn't playing, eating, going for a walk with Mummy and the twins, or thinking about other things, Jeremy James thought about bills. If Daddy didn't have bills, he would be richer. And if Daddy were richer, Jeremy James might get more pocket money. But how could Jeremy James save Daddy from paying bills?

It was when Jeremy James was helping Mummy in the garden that the seed of an idea sowed itself in his mind. They were pulling up weeds, which they were throwing into a rubbish bag.

'Weeds,' said Mummy, 'are a nuisance.'

'Are they a worple worple nuisance?' asked Jeremy James.

'Yes,' said Mummy.

'Then they're just like bills,' said Jeremy James.

That night, before he went to sleep, Jeremy James thought long and hard about Daddy and bills and rubbish bags. He remembered that only yesterday Daddy had bitten into an apple which had had a maggot in it, and Daddy had thrown it in the rubbish. ('Thank heaven,' said Daddy, 'it wasn't *half* a maggot.') If bad things were thrown away, why didn't Daddy throw his bills away?

The next morning, when Jeremy James went downstairs, Daddy was in the kitchen searching for something.

'You haven't seen the sugar, have you, Jeremy James?' asked Daddy.

'I saw Mummy pour sugar into that blue tin,' said Jeremy James.

'Ah yes,' said Daddy, 'the sugar tin. I didn't think of that.'

Of course! Daddy would never think of looking for sugar in the sugar tin, or for shoes in the shoe cupboard or clothes in the clothes cupboard. So why should he think of throwing bills in the rubbish bag?

Jeremy James thought of telling Daddy about his bright idea, but grown-ups sometimes didn't understand bright ideas. They certainly hadn't understood his clever way of beating Melissa at 'Freezing'. And they hadn't understood why he'd once stopped a train, and once fed an elephant, and once taken a tin of mandarin oranges from the bottom of the pile. No, he had better keep his bright idea to himself and see what he could do without the grown-ups.

That morning there were two letters. One was

hand-written, and Jeremy James gave it to Mummy. The other was printed and brown, and Jeremy James took it up to his bedroom and buried it under a pile of cars and planes and books and trains.

'Nothing for me?' asked Daddy.

'Nothing,' said Jeremy James.

Daddy didn't seem pleased that there was nothing for him, but on the other hand he didn't say, 'Ugh!'

As the days stretched into weeks, so the pile of hidden letters grew bigger and bigger. Jeremy James wondered how much money he'd already saved Daddy, and he also wondered when a richer Daddy would make a richer Jeremy James.

'Daddy,' he asked one day, 'if you had more money, would you give me more pocket money?'

'I expect so,' said Daddy.

'Well,' said Jeremy James, 'I was just wondering if perhaps you did have more money.'

'More money than what?' asked Daddy.

'More money than before,' said Jeremy James.

'More money than before what?' asked Daddy.

Jeremy James thought for a moment. 'Well, more money than before now,' he said.

Daddy turned to Mummy, who had just come in with a heavy shopping basket.

'Our eldest child,' he said, 'is asking for a rise.'

'I don't blame him,' said Mummy, 'with the price things are today. I'd ask for one myself if we could afford it.'

Jeremy James suggested that they *could* afford it now that they weren't paying any bills, but Daddy simply looked surprised and asked why Jeremy James thought they weren't paying any bills.

'Because,' said Jeremy James, 'I haven't brought you any.'

'Yes, it has been rather a quiet period,' said Daddy. 'They'll probably all come together. Just before Christmas.'

But they didn't all come together. They came one at a time, and one at a time they found their way upstairs to their secret hiding-place. Unfortunately Daddy, who had never realized that bills could be thrown away, still didn't realize that he now had no bills to pay. Nor did he realize that he was richer than he had been before. And so he didn't realize that he could give Jeremy James *and* Mummy a rise. That was the trouble with a Daddy who didn't think of things.

There was a different kind of trouble ahead, though, and it was trouble that made Daddy, Mummy and Jeremy James do quite a lot of thinking. Daddy had gone into town with Jeremy James, leaving Mummy at home with Christopher and Jennifer, and when they had come back they had found Mummy looking even grumblier than Daddy had looked in the days when he used to receive bills.

'What's the matter?' asked Daddy.

'It's the telephone man,' said Mummy. 'They've cut our phone off.'

'Cut our phone off?' cried Daddy.

'They say we haven't paid our bill!' said Mummy.

'Haven't paid our bill?' cried Daddy.

'I told them there must be some mistake,' said Mummy, 'but they said we'd had a bill and a reminder and a final warning!'

'Final warning?' cried Daddy.

'And now they've cut it off,' said Mummy.

Jeremy James didn't quite know what was meant by cutting a phone off, but it sounded very painful indeed.

'We haven't even had a bill, let alone a final warning!' cried Daddy. 'I shall ring them up straight away.'

'You can't,' said Mummy. 'You've nothing to ring them with.'

Jeremy James had a sort of burning feeling behind his eyes, and his heart seemed to have slipped down into his tummy. Perhaps it was time to tell Mummy and Daddy about his bright idea, which might not have been so bright after all.

'Mummy,' he said.

'Yes, dear?' asked Mummy.

'Um . . . if we found the bill, would they stick the phone back on again?'

'If we found it and paid it they would,' said Mummy.

Jeremy James ran upstairs to his room, flung books and planes and cars and trains in all directions, and came downstairs again with an armful of printed brown envelopes.

Daddy's mouth opened and shut as if an elephant had just sat on his car, and Mummy's eyes went as wide and round as a pair of headlights.

'Where on earth did these come from?' Mummy asked.

Jeremy James told them all about his bright idea which might not have been so bright. When he had finished, there was a long silence. At last Daddy reached down, took all the brown envelopes, and said:

'I've told you before about these bright ideas, Jeremy James. In future, would you please speak before you act.'

'The trouble is,' said Mummy, 'if you don't pay your bills, you can't have any more light or heat or phone or even your house. They'll all get taken away, Jeremy James.'

'I didn't know that,' said Jeremy James.

'You didn't think,' said Daddy. 'I suppose you

meant well, but you just didn't think. Now I'd better go and write out some cheques.'

With a grumbly face he went into his study and closed the door behind him.

'Next time you get a bright idea, Jeremy James,' said Mummy, 'you'll tell us, won't you?'

'Yes, Mummy,' said Jeremy James.

Daddy opened his study door.

'You haven't seen my chequebook, have you?' he asked.

'Probably in your jacket,' said Mummy. 'In a leather case marked *chequebook*.'

'Ah,' said Daddy. 'Thanks. I didn't think of that.'

CHAPTER NINE

The Magician

'Now watch carefully!' said The Great Marvello.

Jeremy James watched carefully.

'You see this empty cone?'

Jeremy James saw the empty cone.

'You see this black cloth?'

Jeremy James saw the black cloth.

'I place this black cloth . . . nothing in it, you see, just a plain black cloth . . . over the empty cone . . . so. I pick up the cone . . . so . . . I pass the cloth through the cone . . . and out . . . comes . . .'

And out came one, two, three white doves, which fluttered into the air and came to rest on the magician's outstretched arm.

Jeremy James gasped, and Mummy and Daddy applauded.

'How did he do it, Mummy?' asked Jeremy James.

'No idea,' said Mummy.

'How did he do it, Daddy?' asked Jeremy James.

'Couldn't tell you,' said Daddy.

'Where did the birds come from?' asked Jeremy James, hoping that someone in the hall would tell him. But nobody else could hear him, apart from

Mummy and Daddy, because the applause was so loud. So Jeremy James waited till the applause had ended. Then he asked again, 'Where did the birds come from?'

A few people laughed, and some heads turned round, and Mummy whispered, 'We don't know, Jeremy James. Let's watch the next trick.'

But The Great Marvello had heard the question, and a little smile glinted from behind the black beard. In his shining black suit and red cape he stepped down from the stage, like a god from a mountain, and walked slowly up the aisle.

'For my next trick,' he announced as he walked, 'I shall need a little help from the audience.'

Jeremy James's eyes became rounder and rounder as the great man approached, and he held his breath with excitement, willing The Great Marvello to come to him.

'I need a man,' said the magician.

Jeremy James wanted to shout out, 'Daddy's a man!' but he couldn't move or speak in the ever nearer presence of the magic Marvello.

'A man and wife,' said the magician. 'Or perhaps a man and child.'

'Me!' cried Jeremy James's voice before he could even think of stopping it.

'Aha!' said the great man, drawing level with Jeremy James.

'Oh Lord!' said Daddy.

'You'd like to help?' Marvello asked Jeremy James.

161

'Yes, please!' said Jeremy James.

'Would you mind, sir?' Marvello asked Daddy.

'Ugh ugh,' said Daddy, 'um . . . well I'd . . .'

'Splendid!' said Marvello. 'A couple of good sports. Come with me then, please.'

A hall full of smiling faces watched as Jeremy James marched up on stage behind Marvello, while Daddy, red-faced, followed several paces behind. They told the magician their names, and then Marvello asked Daddy for his wristwatch.

'Now then, Jeremy James,' said Marvello, 'I want you to look into this paper bag and tell me what you see.'

Jeremy James looked into the paper bag and announced that he could see nothing. Daddy could see nothing either.

'Right,' said Marvello. 'And now I shall put the watch into the paper bag.'

In it went, and he closed the bag, folded over the top, and handed it to Jeremy James.

'Can you still feel the watch in there, Jeremy James?' he asked.

Jeremy James could.

'Now I want you to put the bag under this black cloth,' said the magician.

Jeremy James put the bag with Daddy's watch under the black cloth. Then the magician showed them both another empty bag which Jeremy James had to put under another black cloth on the other side of the table. And so there were now two bags under two cloths, one at either end of the table. Then

from somewhere that Jeremy James didn't see, Marvello produced a very large hammer.

'Oh no!' said Daddy.

'Oh yes!' said Marvello. 'I want you to take this hammer, John, and smash your watch.'

Daddy didn't want to do it, but the magician and Jeremy James both said he should, and so he did. Then Marvello allowed Jeremy James to hammer the watch too, 'just to make sure.' After that he invited Daddy to lift up the black cloth and open the paper bag with his smashed watch in it. This Daddy did, only to find that his watch wasn't there.

'Now, Jeremy James,' said the magician, 'I want you to lift the other cloth and open the other paper bag.'

Inside the other paper bag, what did Jeremy James find? He found Daddy's unsmashed watch.

Everyone in the hall clapped very loudly, and the magician asked them to give Daddy and Jeremy James a special clap as they went back to their seats.

Jeremy James had never seen anything so wonderful as the trick with Daddy's watch. He talked about it all the way home, and at home he told the baby-sitter all about it, and next morning he told Christopher and Jennifer all about it, and next afternoon he told Richard and Trevor all about it. And the day after next, when he met Timothy from next door, he told him all about it too.

'I've seen that trick a dozen times,' said Timothy. 'It's easy.'

'It isn't,' said Jeremy James. 'It's magic.'

'Magic poo,' said Timothy. 'Anyone can do that trick.'

'I'll bet you can't,' said Jeremy James.

'Oh yes I can,' said Timothy.

'All right,' said Jeremy James, 'show me, then.'

Together they went to Timothy's house.

'Hello, Jeremy,' said Mrs Smyth-Fortescue (who never called him Jeremy James). 'Have you come to play with Timothy?'

'Hello, Mrs Smite-Fortytwo,' said Jeremy James, 'Timothy wants to show me a trick.'

'Oh, that's nice,' said Mrs Smyth-Fortescue.

'I want two paper bags,' said Timothy, 'and two bits of cloth.'

'Please,' said Mrs Smyth-Fortescue.

'Now,' said Timothy.

Mrs Smyth-Fortescue provided the paper bags and two tea-towels. Then Timothy himself went to fetch his father's big hammer.

'Oh dear,' said Mrs Smyth-Fortescue, 'that looks a little dangerous.'

'No it isn't,' said Timothy. 'I'm only going to hit a paper bag.'

Timothy led the way upstairs to his room, and there he took off his brand new wristwatch, which his Daddy had just brought back from America. Then he opened the first paper bag and put the watch inside.

'Now put it under the cloth,' said Timothy.

Jeremy James put it under the tea-towel at one end of Timothy's table.

'Now look in the other bag,' said Timothy.

Jeremy James looked in the other bag.

'What's in it?' asked Timothy.

'Nothing,' said Jeremy James.

'Put it under the other cloth,' said Timothy.

Jeremy James put it under the other tea-towel at the other end of Timothy's table.

'Right!' said Timothy. 'Now watch!'

He picked up the hammer and raised it high in the air.

'Are you sure . . .?' Jeremy James started to ask, as Timothy brought the hammer down with a tremendous crash on to the first paper bag.

'You can hit it, too, if you like,' said Timothy generously.

But Jeremy James didn't want to.

'Coward!' said Timothy. 'There's nothing to be scared of.'

Jeremy James wasn't scared. He just had a funny feeling that Timothy shouldn't be doing this trick.

'All right,' said Timothy. 'Have a look in the bag.'

Jeremy James took off the first tea-towel, picked up the first bag, and looked inside. What did he find? He found Timothy's smashed watch.

He showed it to Timothy, whose face went almost as white as Marvello's doves. Timothy grabbed the second bag and opened it. What did he find? He found nothing.

'I've smashed my watch!' said Timothy.

'Yes,' said Jeremy James.

'What was that terrible crash?' asked Mrs Smyth-Fortescue, poking her head round Timothy's door.

'It was Timothy's trick,' said Jeremy James. 'But it didn't work.'

When Jeremy James told Mummy and Daddy about Timothy's trick, they both shook their heads and said, 'Ts! Ts!' and, 'What a silly boy!'

'I expect it was an expensive watch, too,' said Mummy.

'I know why the trick didn't work,' said Jeremy James.

'Why?' asked Daddy.

'Because,' said Jeremy James, 'it was the wrong watch. He should have used Daddy's.'

CHAPTER TEN

The Robbers

'Ugh!' said Daddy. 'Oh dear, oh dear! Hmmph! Ugh!'

Jeremy James had just brought Daddy a long white printed envelope which the postman had popped through the letter box.

'What is it, John?' asked Mummy.

'It's . . . ugh hmmph . . . from the bank manager,' said Daddy.

'Oh dear,' said Mummy.

'He wants me to go and see him,' said Daddy.

'Oh dear, oh dear,' said Mummy.

'It appears,' said Daddy, 'that we are overdrawn.'

'Oh dear, oh dear, oh dear,' said Mummy.

Jeremy James didn't know what 'overdrawn' meant, but it didn't seem a very good thing to be, and when he asked Daddy who had 'overdrawed' him, Daddy pulled a long face and said that he had overdrawed himself.

'It means,' said Mummy, as Daddy *hmmphed* and *ughed* through the letter for the fourth time, 'that we've taken more out of the bank then we've put in. So now we owe the bank some money.'

'I've got 20p in my money box,' said Jeremy

James. 'Though I was going to buy some liquorice allsorts with that.'

'Thanks,' said Daddy, 'but the bank manager wants more than liquorice allsorts, I'm afraid.'

It was decided that Mummy should go shopping with the twins, while Daddy and Jeremy James went to the bank. Then they would meet afterwards and come home together.

'What do banks do?' asked Jeremy James on the way.

'They look after your money,' said Daddy. 'If you have any.'

'Why?' asked Jeremy James.

'So that people can't steal it from you,' said Daddy.

'Can't they steal it from banks?' asked Jeremy James.

Daddy said they could, but it was difficult. Jeremy James wondered if he should ask the bank to look after his 20p, but Daddy reckoned that was too little. Jeremy James said it was more than Daddy had, and if the bank was looking after Daddy's less-than-nothing, it could also look after 20p. Daddy said, 'Hmmph!' and 'Ugh!' and by now they'd reached the bank.

Inside the bank was a queue of people at a long counter, and Jeremy James saw a girl behind the counter giving a thick wad of notes to a bald man in a suit. The man said, 'Thank you,' put the money in his wallet, and walked off.

'Daddy!' cried Jeremy James. 'That lady's giving money away! Why don't we get some from her?'

'I wish we could,' said Daddy, 'but it's like your money-box – what doesn't go in can't come out.'

Daddy went up to a young lady at the very end of the counter and asked her something.

'I'll see if he's free,' said the young lady, and Daddy and Jeremy James sat down on two chairs in the corner.

'How do you steal from a bank?' asked Jeremy James.

'The usual way,' said Daddy, 'is to get a gun and say "stick 'em up". But I wouldn't try it if I were you.'

The young lady opened a door in the end wall.

'Mr Stoneheart will see you now,' she said.

'Right,' said Daddy. 'You wait here, Jeremy James. I shan't be long.'

Daddy straightened his tie, gave a little cough, took a deep breath, and passed through the door in the end wall.

Jeremy James sat watching the queue of people at the long counter. Some gave money in, and some took money out, and there seemed to be a lot more taker-outers than giver-inners. It might not be a bad idea, thought Jeremy James, to go and join the queue, just to see if he could be one of the taker-outers. That would give Daddy a nice surprise.

Jeremy James was about to jump down from his chair when he suddenly saw something that made him pause. The something that he saw was two young

men who had just joined the queue. Jeremy James
would have had to stand behind them, and he decided
at once that he didn't want to stand anywhere near
them. One had a lot of black bristle on his face, while
the other had a scarf over his mouth and chin, and
they both wore dirty raincoats and looked very rough.

Slowly they moved towards the head of the queue.
The bristly man put a cigarette in his mouth and gave
one to the scarfy man. Then the bristly man reached
into his raincoat pocket and brought out ... Jeremy
James's eyes went as round as 10p pieces. The bristly
man was holding a gun.

If you want to steal from a bank, Daddy had said,
get a gun. But if you don't want them to steal from
a bank, thought Jeremy James, get Daddy.

He walked boldly to the door in the end wall, turned the handle, and went in.

A grey-haired man with a grey moustache and a grey suit was sitting opposite the door behind a desk, and Daddy was sitting with his back to the door, saying, 'Er . . . worple . . . um . . . ugh . . .'

'Hello,' said the grey-haired man, 'what's this?'

Daddy turned round.

'Oh!' he said. 'Um . . . this is my son. What is it, Jeremy James?'

'There are two men with guns in the bank,' said Jeremy James.

'*Two men with guns?*' echoed the grey-haired man.

'Now hold on, Jeremy James,' said Daddy, 'are you sure . . .'

'*Are you sure?*' echoed the grey-haired man.

'Oh yes,' said Jeremy James, 'they've come to steal from the bank.'

The grey-haired man pressed a button on his desk, leapt out of his chair, banged his knee on a sharp corner, said a word Mummy had absolutely forbidden, limped to a door in the far wall and hurried out.

'Are you sure they had guns?' asked Daddy.

'Well, one of them did,' said Jeremy James. 'And the other one had a scarf.'

'He'll have a job holding up the bank with a scarf,' said Daddy.

Suddenly bells started ringing, and from inside the bank Daddy and Jeremy James heard someone shouting. Jeremy James wanted to open the door so they could see what was happening, but Daddy said they must stay where they were in case the gunman started shooting, or the scarfman started scarfing.

Then the bells stopped ringing, and everything was very quiet.

'Everything's very quiet,' said Daddy.

'Can we have a look?' asked Jeremy James.

'No,' said Daddy. 'It may be a gun with a silencer.'

They waited and waited, until at last the bank manager came back with a policeman, who looked very tall and very serious.

'This,' said the bank manager, 'is the young man who gave the alarm. And this is the young man's father.'

'Morning, sir,' said the policeman.

'Um . . . good morning, Officer,' said Daddy.

'What's your name, son?' asked the policeman.

'Jeremy James,' said Jeremy James.

'Well, Jeremy James,' said the policeman, 'the two men you saw were not here to rob the bank.'

'Oh dear,' said Daddy.

'And what you thought was a gun,' said the policeman, 'was a cigarette lighter.'

'Oh dear, oh dear,' said Daddy, 'I'm extremely sorry, but . . .'

'However,' said the policeman.

'However?' said Daddy.

'Although they weren't here to rob the bank,' said the policeman, 'they happen to be two villains that we've been after for quite some time. And as a matter of fact, there is a substantial reward for information leading to their capture.'

'A reward?' echoed Daddy.

'A substantial reward,' said the policeman. 'You've got a smart lad there, sir. You can be proud of him.'

'I certainly am,' said Daddy.

Then they all went out into the bank itself, and people crowded round Jeremy James and said what a smart lad he was. Jeremy James had a feeling that he wasn't so smart, since the bank robbers hadn't really been bank robbers at all, but he didn't tell anyone he wasn't so smart, because he wasn't so stupid.

'Now about that overdraft of yours,' said the bank manager when all the fuss had ended and the policeman had gone and the people had moved away. 'I'm sure you'll put it right in no time.'

'Yes, of course,' said Daddy.

'So let's forget about it, shall we?' said the bank manager.

'I'll be pleased to,' said Daddy.

The bank manager accompanied them all the way to the door of the bank, shook them both by the hand, and told them – with his last words of farewell – that the bank would always be at their service.

Daddy and Jeremy James met Mummy and the twins as planned, but they didn't go straight home. They stopped at the coffee-shop, and Jeremy James was allowed to choose any piece of cake he liked. Then, while he sat and ate his chocolate gateau and

drank his Coca Cola, Daddy told Mummy the whole
story.

'Well done, Jeremy James,' said Mummy.

'So what do you think of banks?' asked Daddy.

Jeremy James thought for a moment. After all, if
it *had* been a gun and if he hadn't been there, the
two men could easily have taken all the money out
of the bank.

'Banks are all right,' he said, 'but I think I'll keep
my 20p at home.'

CHAPTER ELEVEN

Mr Blooming

It was snowing. The world through the window was a moving blur of dots and flickers, just like the television set when Daddy was trying to adjust it. Slowly everything was turning white, and yet even when the snowflakes brushed against the glass, they made no noise. They were silent and magical, like a ghost painting.

'What *is* snow?' asked Jeremy James.

'A blooming nuisance,' said Daddy.

'It's a sort of rain that freezes and falls from the sky,' said Mummy.

'It looks nice,' said Jeremy James.

'So does the river,' said Daddy. 'Until you fall in it.'

'You can go out and play in it if you like,' said Mummy.

'No thank you,' said Daddy.

'Yes please,' said Jeremy James.

And so Jeremy James was wrapped up in a coat, scarf and gloves, with wellington boots down below and woollen hat on top. Then he stepped out on to the ankle-deep carpet that was the back garden.

The snow was still falling, and one or two flakes touched his face. They were as cool as ice cream, and he wondered what flavour they were. He opened his mouth and tilted his head back till a snowflake fell in. There was no flavour at all. Just a quick, cold tingle.

'I wish they made strawberry-flavour snow,' said Jeremy James.

He scrunched through the garden leaving giant footprints behind him, and then he scrunched back to make the footprints even more giant. After that he threw handfuls of snow at nothing in particular, and found that most of it either blew back in his face or trickled down his wrists and into his sleeves or gloves. It was very wet.

'Having fun?' asked Daddy's voice.

Jeremy James hadn't even heard Daddy coming, but there he stood, as muffled up as Jeremy James and eyes shining just as brightly.

'How would you like to build a snowman?' he asked.

'Yes please,' said Jeremy James.

'Great!' said Daddy. 'I haven't built a snowman since I was a boy.'

Jeremy James laughed.

'You weren't a boy, were you, Daddy?'

'Of course I was,' said Daddy.

'Funny,' said Jeremy James. 'I don't remember that.'

Jeremy James and Daddy set to work building a pile of snow. Daddy packed it all tightly together so that it was really hard, and Jeremy James kept bringing handfuls to pat into the pile Daddy had made.

Gradually it grew taller and taller, and eventually Daddy stood back and said:

'Right, that's the body. Now for the head.'

'Where are his legs?' asked Jeremy James.

'Ah!' said Daddy. 'Well he's wearing a long white coat.'

Jeremy James looked hard at the pile, and it *did* look a bit like a long white coat. But even a man in a long white coat would have arms.

'Ah!' said Daddy. 'Well his arms are behind his back.'

Jeremy James looked hard at the pile, and it *did* look a bit like a man with arms behind his back.

'Let's do his head,' said Daddy.

Together they rolled up a big ball, lifted it and stuck it on top of the pile.

'There we are,' said Daddy. 'That's the head.'

'Where are his eyes and nose and mouth?' asked Jeremy James.

'You'll make a good critic,' said Daddy. 'But you're right – he *has* got a rather blank expression.'

Two pebbles, a clothes peg and an old clay pipe soon changed that, and Jeremy James found himself looking at a bald-headed man in a long white coat with his arms behind his back.

'How does he look?' asked Daddy.

'He looks cold,' said Jeremy James.

'Right again,' said Daddy, and put his hat on the

snowman's head and his scarf round the snowman's neck.

'Now *you* look cold,' said Jeremy James.

'What are we going to call him?' asked Daddy.

Jeremy James thought for a moment.

'Mr Blooming,' he said.

'Why Mr Blooming?' asked Daddy.

'Because he's made of blooming snow,' said Jeremy James.

Jeremy James was very proud of Mr Blooming (and so was Daddy), and he looked out at him from the living room window several times during the day, just to make sure he was still there. And he *was* still there, calmly smoking his pipe and looking up at the house with his arms behind his back.

'Can we give him something to eat?' Jeremy James asked Mummy.

'I don't think he'd like our food,' said Mummy.

'I'll bet he likes strawberry ice cream,' said Jeremy James.

But Mummy thought it was too cold for ice cream.

'Then can we give him some soup?' asked Jeremy James.

'Soup isn't good for snowmen,' said Mummy.

'It's only good for Soupermen,' said Daddy.

'Well what *can* we give him?' asked Jeremy James.

But Mummy and Daddy said there was nothing they could give him, because snowmen didn't eat and didn't drink anything except snow.

Just before he went to bed, Jeremy James crept into the twins' bedroom and looked out of their window. It had stopped snowing. Mr Blooming was standing in the middle of the white lawn, and Jeremy James waved to him.

'I hope you won't get hungry in the night,' he whispered.

Next morning, Jeremy James woke up and looked out of his window. Most of the snow had gone. He rushed into the twins' room.

'Jem Jem!' cried Jennifer, pulling herself to her feet.

But Jeremy James didn't have time to talk to Jennifer. He ran straight to the window. Mr Blooming was still there – but somehow he looked different. There was some green grass around him now, but it wasn't the green that had changed him. No, he was smaller – his head had sunk, and the hat had fallen over his face.

'I knew he'd get hungry!' cried Jeremy James, and ran downstairs.

Mummy was in the kitchen.

'Good morning, Jeremy James,' she said. 'You're bright and early. What's the matter?'

'It's Mr Blooming!' said Jeremy James. 'He's hungry.'

Mummy looked out of the window.

'I'm afraid he's melting,' she said.

'No, he needs some snow,' said Jeremy James. 'He wants his breakfast!'

Mummy helped Jeremy James get dressed quickly, and out he raced into the garden.

'I'm coming, Mr Blooming!' he cried, and stooped to pick up a handful of snow. But the snow was not like yesterday's – it was soft and mushy, and dripped through Jeremy James's fingers. He carried what was left of it to Mr Blooming, and pressed it against his mouth, but all that happened was that the pipe fell out, and the breakfast snow simply dripped on to Mr Blooming's scarf.

Jeremy James could see now that Mr Blooming's body had shrunk to only half the size it had been.

'It's no good, I'm afraid,' said Mummy's voice

behind him. 'Once snow starts to melt, there's nothing you can do.'

Gently she tipped Mr Blooming's hat back so that it wasn't over his eyes.

'Snow is only water, you see,' she said.

'Maybe he'd eat some ice cream,' said Jeremy James. 'Ice cream is like snow, Mummy, isn't it?'

'I'll tell you what,' said Mummy. 'You can give him a spoonful of ice cream, and if he eats it, you can give him some more.'

She went back into the kitchen, and brought out the tub of ice cream and a spoon. But when Jeremy James tried to put the spoon into Mr Blooming's mouth, the ice cream fell off and plopped on to the ground below.

'He won't eat it,' said Jeremy James.

'No,' said Mummy. 'Snowmen only eat snow.'

Sadly Jeremy James went back into the house with Mummy. But all through breakfast he gazed out of the window at Mr Blooming. It didn't make him feel any better either when Daddy came into the room.

'Not a bad morning. At least the blooming snow has gone.'

Mummy pointed silently towards Jeremy James and then towards the garden. Daddy put his hand to his mouth and murmured, 'Sorry!' Then Mummy went upstairs to see to the twins, and Daddy sat down beside Jeremy James.

'I've been thinking,' he said. 'Next time it snows, we'll build a proper snowman. We'll buy a mask to

use as a face, and we'll give him a jacket so that he's
got arms. What do you think, Jeremy James?'

'Mr Blooming *is* a proper snowman,' said Jeremy
James.

'Well, yes, he is,' said Daddy. 'But the next one
will be even more proper.'

'When's it going to snow again?' asked Jeremy
James.

'I don't know,' said Daddy. 'But if you get yourself
ready, we'll go and buy that mask now, in case it
snows tomorrow.'

By the time Jeremy James and Daddy came back from
town with their mask and with a bag of shopping for
Mummy, there was very little of Mr Blooming left:

just a tiny ball of snow, a hat and a scarf, two pebbles, a peg and a pipe. Jeremy James and Daddy stood looking sadly down.

'Daddy,' said Jeremy James, 'will I melt like that one day?'

Daddy thought for a moment.

'Do you drink soup?' he asked.

'Yes,' said Jeremy James.

'And do you eat ice cream?'

'Yes,' said Jeremy James.

'Then you won't melt,' said Daddy. 'At least not for a very long time.'

CHAPTER TWELVE

Cold Nativity

'I thick I cad see a star,' said Jeremy James.

'Oh dear,' creaked the voice of the Reverend Cole as the Reverend Cole creaked towards the platform. 'Can't you say "think" and ... um ... "can"?'

'Do,' said Jeremy James. 'I've got a code.'

'Oh dear,' said the Reverend Cole again, 'a shepherd with a cold. Well, do ... um ... the best you can.'

'I thick I cad see a star,' said Jeremy James, 'shidig over Bethleheb.'

'Over where?' cried the Reverend Cole.

'Bethleheb,' said Jeremy James.

It was the dress rehearsal of the Sunday School Nativity Play, and Jeremy James wasn't enjoying it very much. Nor was the Reverend Cole. His shepherd was not the only one with a cold – Joseph had one as well. And his was so bad that he hadn't even come to the rehearsal. A Nativity Play without Joseph is rather like stuffing without turkey. The Virgin Mary was there all right, and so was the baby Jesus, which being a china doll had managed to avoid catching a cold. But there were only two wise men, and one of

185

those was little Trevor who, for a wise man, had a terrible memory and could never remember any of his six lines.

Jeremy James had a very good memory. His memory was so good that he knew almost every line of the whole play. But no matter what line he spoke today, it was full of sniffs and d's and b's.

Fat Richard, who was the inn-keeper, also had a cold, and when he informed Mary that there was 'no roob at the idd', the Reverend Cole sat down in a pew, put his head in his hands, and groaned.

'We can't go on!' he cried.

The Reverend Cole was very old, and very tired. He had produced a Nativity Play every Christmas for the last thirty-five years, but now he vowed that the thirty-sixth would be his last. There had, of course, been disasters in the past. Once he had lost Joseph to a flu epidemic and had actually taken the part himself (which he enjoyed, because he liked acting) – but there had never been a rehearsal quite as disastrous as this one. The Nativity, he reckoned, would be the death of him.

'It's no good!' he cried. 'Everybody go home, wrap up warm, take vitamin C, and pray for a miracle. I want you back here at nine o'clock in the morning for a final run-through.'

Mummy was waiting for Jeremy James at the back of the church.

'How did it go?' she asked.

'Dot very well,' said Jeremy James. 'Bister Cole wasert very pleased, add we have to go back toborrow at dide o'clock.'

By nine o'clock the following morning, some of the Reverend Cole's prayers had been answered. There had indeed been one or two miracles. For one thing, his Joseph was there and ready to do his part. For another, the third wise man was there as well. And the Lord had also been merciful to Richard and to Jeremy James, because both of them were now able to say 'Bethlehem' and 'inn'.

With such blessings, one might have thought that the Reverend Cole's problem were over. However, Joseph's return had been balanced by the Virgin Mary's absence. Sarah Goody had been struck down by illness, and under no circumstances would her parents allow her to leave her bed since she had been so sick in the night.

The recovery of the other actors had to be paid for by the Reverend Cole himself. By nine o'clock his aged eyes were streaming, his old nose was blocked, and he was cursing himself for not having retired last year.

If a Nativity Play without Joseph is like stuffing without turkey, a Nativity Play without the Virgin Mary is like Christmas dinner without turkey, stuffing, *and* Christmas pudding. The situation was hopeless. Not even the Reverend Cole could possibly pass for the Virgin Mary.

'It's do good,' he said to the children. 'We cart go od without a Virgid Bary.'

'I could be the Virgin Mary,' said Jeremy James.

'You?' exclaimed the Reverend Cole.

'I know the lines,' said Jeremy James.

'It's true,' said Richard. 'He knows everybody's part.'

The Reverend Cole's watery eyes opened wide behind his glasses. It was as if he had suddenly seen a bright star over the High Street.

'Do you really dow the lides?' he asked.

Jeremy James recited some of the lines, and the Reverend Cole rubbed his hands like a shepherd on a cold winter's night.

'Try od the costube, thed,' he said.

The Virgin Mary's costume fitted Jeremy James perfectly.

'This is really quite rebarkable,' said the Reverend Cole. 'Truly the Lord works id bysterious ways.'

'Please, Mr Cole,' asked Jeremy James, 'will I be the shepherd as well?'

'Ah, do,' said the Reverend Cole. 'I thick I'd better play that part byself.'

The run-through went quite well. Jeremy James forgot his lines twice, and Trevor forgot his three times, and Richard accidentally bumped into the crib and sent baby Jesus flying across the platform, but otherwise there were no disasters.

The performance was due to start at three o'clock, and so all the actors had to be back by half-past one, in order to leave time for make-up, last minute adjustments to costumes, and last minute adjustments to the Reverend Cole's prayers. To his relief, everyone came punctually, and all he had to pray for was the Lord's goodwill, which he knew he had already.

At five-to-three, the Reverend Cole announced to a packed church that as Sarah Goody had fallen ill, the part of the Virgin Mary had been taken over at the last minute by Jeremy James. The part of the shepherd would . . . um . . . be played by 'byself'.

Jeremy James peeped out into the church, and murmured to Richard that there were lots and lots of people there. Richard turned a little pale and said he was sure to forget some of his lines. Trevor turned even paler and said he was sure to forget all of his lines.

Jeremy James was dressed in a long costume with a shawl and a headscarf. He had red lips and red cheeks, and Mrs Grundy, who had made him up, had said he was the prettiest Virgin Mary she'd ever seen.

(And Mrs Grundy had been making up Virgin Marys almost as long as the Reverend Cole had been directing them.) Jeremy James wasn't altogether sure that he *wanted* to be pretty, but on the whole he thought it better to be a pretty Virgin Mary than a cold shepherd.

The Reverend Cole came backstage.

'Right!' he whispered. 'Let's begid.'

When Jeremy James went out on to the platform with Peter Cutting, who was Joseph, he had quite a few lines to say straight away, and he said them all without making a single mistake. Then there was a passage while other people were speaking, and he had a look round the church. He spotted Mummy and Daddy and the twins sitting in the third row, and gave them a quick wave. Mummy waved back. (The Reverend Cole had told them not to wave at anyone, but the Reverend Cole was backstage, so he wouldn't know.)

Richard, as the inn-keeper, was very nervous, and when he forgot his words, Jeremy James whispered them to him.

'What?' said Richard.

Jeremy James said them a bit louder, and then Richard said, 'thank you' and repeated what Jeremy James had told him. But he couldn't remember the next words either, so Jeremy James had to tell him again.

The next scene was the shepherd's, and the Reverend Cole remembered all his words very well. But one or two people in the church giggled when he said, 'I thick I cad see a star shidig over Bethleheb.'

Trevor forgot his lines several times. But nobody noticed because he spoke so softly that even Jeremy James could hardly hear him, although they were next to each other on the platform.

In spite of everything, the play was a great success, and there were no disasters at all. At the end everybody clapped, and there was an especially loud clap for the Virgin Mary, who smiled straight at Mummy and Daddy, who smiled back.

Then the Reverend Cole made a little speech, in which he congratulated all the children, said how hard they'd worked and what a pleasure it had been to produce the play, and he was now looking forward to producing one again next year. He finished by saying:

'I'd like to bake a special bedtion of Jereby Jabes who . . . ub . . . acted the Virgid Bary at just a few hours' dotice. Well dud . . . ub . . . Jereby Jabes.'

Then he let out a loud sneeze, and everybody said, 'Bless you.'

'Add bless you, too,' said the Reverend Cole.

Please Keep Off the Dinosaur

For Helmut Winter,
who started it all

Contents

CHAPTER ONE

Hello, London

'Is London bigger than the High Street?' asked Jeremy James.

'Much bigger,' said Daddy.

'How much bigger?' asked Jeremy James.

'Hugely bigger,' said Daddy. 'It's bigger than the High Street by as much as an elephant is bigger than a piece of cheese.'

Jeremy James gasped. 'Then it must be hugely huge.'

'It is,' said Daddy.

'And it must have lots of toy shops.'

'Hundreds.'

'And lots of sweet shops.'

'Thousands.'

'Can we go to all of them?' asked Jeremy James.

'There are other things in life and London,' said Mummy, 'than toy shops and sweet shops. Now finish your breakfast, or by the time you get to London, it'll be time to come home.'

Jeremy James and Daddy were going to London to see an important lady. ('Is she the Queen, Daddy?'

'Well, not quite. She's Mrs Robinson.') They would spend the rest of the day seeing the sights, and would spend the night in a hotel before driving back tomorrow. The name of the hotel, much to Jeremy James's delight, was Hotel Jeremy. Daddy had chosen it specially because, he said, a hotel with a name like that just had to be nice.

Mummy would have liked to go to London, too, but decided that it wouldn't be much fun wheeling the twins around all day.

'Jeffer go Londy,' suggested Jennifer.

'Another time,' said Mummy.

'Kwiffer Londy,' suggested Christopher, hoping it was something to eat.

'Not today,' said Mummy.

She would take them to the park instead. It wasn't so far.

London was a very long way away, and so Daddy wanted to leave as early as possible. Mummy had already packed Jeremy James's bag, and soon he was all ready to go, smartly dressed, hair neatly combed, face freshly washed, and teeth whitely brushed. It took Daddy a little longer to get ready. First he couldn't find some important papers that he was to give to the important lady. Then he couldn't find the important lady's address. When he found the important papers and the important lady's address, he couldn't find his street map of London, and when he'd found the map, he couldn't find the car keys. Daddy was very bad at finding things, though he said

this was only because he was so good at losing them.
Mummy found the car keys in the medicine cupboard. They should have been in Daddy's jacket,
but they weren't. There were some headache pills in
Daddy's jacket.

'Shouldn't these have been in the medicine cupboard?' asked Daddy.

Eventually, Jeremy James was strapped into the
back seat of the car, and with cheery waves and loud
goodbyes, he and Daddy drove off down the street,
swung round the corner, and glided slowly and
silently to a halt.

'I knew there was something I had to do last
night,' said Daddy.

'What was that?' asked Jeremy James.

'Get some petrol,' said Daddy.

Later, Jeremy James and Daddy found themselves in a long grey street with a line of cars ahead of them and a line of cars behind them, and none of the cars were moving.

'Have they all run out of petrol, Daddy?' asked Jeremy James.

'No,' said Daddy, 'they've run out of room. This is London.'

'But if London's bigger than the High Street,' said Jeremy James, 'there should be lots of room.'

'There is,' said Daddy, 'but none of it is where the cars are.'

The cars all moved forward a few feet and then stopped again. The car next to Daddy's was being driven by a bristly man who suddenly got out, waved his fist, and said some words which sounded like some words nobody was supposed to say.

'What's he saying, Daddy?' asked Jeremy James.

'Something like: "Oh dear me, I fear I shall be late",' replied Daddy.

'He didn't say that,' said Jeremy James.

'Well, he may have put in a few worple worples,' said Daddy.

The traffic did eventually get moving, but it wasn't very long before Daddy began to wonder where they were moving to. Somehow the streets of

London seemed to have shifted from where they'd been on the street map. What should have been a left turn must have been a right turn, or what should have been a right turn must have been a left turn, or maybe they shouldn't have turned at all and oh dear it's a one-way street.

As Daddy lefted, righted, scratched his head and worpled, Jeremy James saw something he'd already seen before — which was a little surprising since this was his first trip to London.

'I know that sweet shop!' he cried.

'I expect you do,' said Daddy. 'We passed it five minutes ago.'

At last they turned into a street that was full of houses without any shops, and there Daddy spotted a lady in a uniform. He pulled up beside her.

'Excuse me!' said Daddy.

'You can't stop here,' said the lady.

'I know,' said Daddy. 'But I'm looking for Welbeck Street.'

'You're in it,' said the lady. 'But you can't stop. You're on a double yellow line.'

'Can you tell me where the nearest car park is?' asked Daddy.

'I can,' said the lady, 'but you won't be able to park there.'

'Why not?' asked Daddy.

'It's full,' said the lady.

'Where can I park, then?' asked Daddy.

'Follow any signs that say "Car Park",' said the lady. 'And hope for the best.'

Off they drove again, through streets where there was no parking, past parks with space and no cars, and past car parks with cars and no space.

Finally they came to a flashing sign, Daddy let out a cry of triumph, and they drove down a dark twisting tunnel, past rows and rows of parked cars, and eventually into a space that was just right for Daddy's car.

'Now I know,' said Daddy, 'how Columbus felt when he discovered America.'

They left the car in its special space, left their cases in the car, and walked out into the grey daylight. Jeremy James noticed that the street was full of paper bags, bent tin cans, newspapers and cigarette packets.

'Are we near the rubbish dump?' he asked.

'No,' said Daddy. 'We're in it.'

They now had to find Welbeck Street again. Daddy took out his street map, turned it upside down, looked left, looked right, and looked lost.

'Can I 'elp yer?' asked a shabby little man with a stubbly chin.

'I'm looking for Welbeck Street,' said Daddy.

'Then I can't 'elp yer,' said the shabby little man, and walked on.

By the time a kindly policeman had shown them the way to Welbeck Street, Mrs Robinson – the important lady – had gone to another appointment, but she had left a message: she would meet Daddy and Jeremy James for lunch the next day, if they were still going to be in London.

'Judging by today's experiences,' said Daddy, 'we'll be lucky if we ever get *out* of London.'

CHAPTER TWO

Wax and 20p

After lunch (chicken and chips, ice cream, and Coca-Cola), Daddy said they were very near to a place called Madame Tussaud's, which was full of wax-work figures of famous people. Jeremy James thought it sounded boring, but it had just started to rain, and Daddy said he'd rather be bored and dry than interested and wet.

No sooner were they inside than Daddy seemed already to have lost his way.

'There's a policeman over there,' he said. 'Just go and ask him where the Chamber of Horrors is.'

Jeremy James went up to the policeman.

'Excuse me,' he said.

The policeman looked straight ahead.

'Could you please tell me the way to the Chamber of Horace?'

The policeman told him nothing.

'Excuse me,' said Jeremy James again.

The policeman didn't even excuse him. Daddy came up beside Jeremy James, and started laughing.

'He's a waxwork!' said Daddy. 'You're talking to a model!'

Jeremy James stood there amazed, gazing at the model of a policeman which looked just like a *real* policeman. To make sure, he pulled the policeman's jacket, and then touched the policeman's hand. It was cold and hard.

'Was he ever a real policeman?' asked Jeremy James.

'No,' said Daddy. 'Just a lump of wax.'

Madame Tussaud's was full of people who weren't people. It was also full of people who *were* people. And so when they'd looked at some of the people who weren't people, Daddy suggested they should get away from all the people who were people, and go to somewhere that was less crowded.

'What about the Chamber of Horace?' asked Jeremy James.

Daddy said this was full of murderers and witches and gruesome, horrible things that Jeremy James shouldn't see, and so Jeremy James said he wanted to see them. Daddy said they'd give him bad dreams, Jeremy James said he liked having bad dreams, and Daddy said, oh all right then, and it couldn't be worse than driving through London.

In the Chamber of Horrors, some of the people who weren't people had rather nasty faces, but so did some of the people who *were* people. There were also some bloodstained instruments and chopped-off heads and people with bulging eyes and hanging-out tongues. They were just like some of the pictures in Jeremy James's giant book of fairy tales.

'Ug, ugh, yuck, look at that!' gasped Daddy, pointing to a bloodstained woman holding a bloodstained knife over a bloodstained man in a bloodstained bath.

'You shouldn't look at it, Daddy!' said Jeremy James. 'It'll give you bad dreams.'

Daddy had soon had enough of frightening himself, and so he and Jeremy James left Madame Tussaud's to join the thousands of real people out on the streets of London. It was still raining, and Daddy said they would take the underground, which was a railway that was underneath the streets. Jeremy James thought this was another of Daddy's jokes, like the policeman-who-wasn't-a-policeman, but Daddy said it was true, and held Jeremy James's hand as they went down a long, moving, rattling staircase. When they reached the bottom, they walked along a rounded, white-tiled passage in which a stragglyhaired young man was playing a guitar and singing in a voice that rattled just like the moving staircase. Daddy gave Jeremy James 20p to drop in the young man's hat, and the young man winked and nodded.

Jeremy James put his hand back in Daddy's, but he was frowning as they walked. An idea was forming in his mind. He waited until they could no longer hear the young man's rattling song, and then he suddenly took his hand out of Daddy's, ran to the

white-tiled side of the passage, and sang at the top of his voice:

'London's burning, London's burning. Fetch the engines, fetch the engines. Fire, fire! Fire, fire . . .'

'Jeremy James!' cried Daddy. 'What on earth are you doing?'

'I'm singing,' said Jeremy James.

'I can hear that,' said Daddy. 'What for?'

'So I can get 20p,' said Jeremy James.

Daddy laughed, and so did some of the people who were hurrying by, but nobody gave Jeremy James 20p. Jeremy James wondered why, and Daddy said maybe it was because people in London weren't too keen to hear that London was burning.

CHAPTER THREE

The Pigeon Lady

The moving staircase, the 20p singer, and the top of Jeremy James's voice had been whispers compared to the mighty roar of the underground train as it had come out of its tunnel. Like the rest of London it had been full of people, and Jeremy James had found himself nose to knees with a dozen different pairs of legs before at last Daddy said it was time to get off.

It had stopped raining now, and Daddy and Jeremy James walked along a crowded pavement until they came to a huge square. It was elephantly bigger than the market square at home. Cars, buses and lorries roared all round it, there were grand buildings on every side, and towering over it was a very tall pillar on top of which stood the figure of a man. Round the pillar were four stone lions.

'This,' said Daddy, 'is Trafalgar Square. And the man on the pillar is Nelson, who won a great victory for England.'

'Was he a footballer?' asked Jeremy James.

'No,' said Daddy, 'he was a sailor. A great admiral, who won a sea battle against the French.'

'Why did they put him on top of a pillar?' asked Jeremy James.

'As a reward for saving England,' said Daddy.

Jeremy James frowned. Being stuck on a pillar seemed to him more of a punishment than a reward. But it was typical of grown-ups to put Nelson on a pillar when he'd probably have been much happier eating a tub of ice cream and going out to play.

The square was full of people and pigeons. Some of the people were feeding some of the pigeons, and one old lady had them all over her, on her head and arms and shoulders. She was throwing pieces of bread on the ground, or holding them out for the pigeons to come and take, and she was smiling all the time and talking to the birds:

'Come on, my beauties,' she was saying. 'Come an' fill yer tums at Auntie Dot's.'

She caught sight of the wide-eyed Jeremy James.

' 'Ere y'are, sonny,' she said. 'Feed the birds. You be nice ter them, an' they'll be nice ter you.'

Jeremy James looked at Daddy, who smiled and nodded, and the old lady gave him a handful of crumbs.

'Just 'old out yer 'ands an' they'll come,' she said.

And come they did. In no time, a dozen birds had gathered round, on and over Jeremy James. One even landed on his wrist and pecked the crumbs out of his hand. The pigeons were all making a gentle cooing noise, and one sat on Jeremy James's head and sang roocoo, roocoo in his ear.

Then Jeremy James felt something warm and soft slipping down the side of his face.

'Oh!' said Daddy.

'Eek!' said Jeremy James.

The something fell with a little plop on to Jeremy James's collar. It was white and sticky.

'What is it?' asked Jeremy James.

'Well,' said Daddy, 'it's normally known as "droppings". But in pigeon English it's sometimes called "Number Coo".'

'That'll bring yer luck, sonny!' said the old lady, and gave Daddy a tissue.

'And what do they do to you if you're unlucky?' asked Daddy.

The old lady laughed.

Daddy tried to wipe Jeremy James's face, but the pigeons were still fluttering all round him. The old lady told him to throw the rest of his crumbs away, and then the pigeons would leave him alone.

'They're jus' like some people,' she said. 'All over yer so long as yer've got somethin' ter give 'em. Not so keen when yer empty-'anded.'

But even when the pigeons had fluttered away, the sticky white stuff still stuck to Jeremy James's collar. The old lady pointed to a fountain across the square.

'A drop o' water's all yer need,' she said. 'Then 'e'll be as clean as a pigeon in a packet o' Persil.'

Daddy took Jeremy James to the fountain, and

washed his face and collar till all the sticky white stuff had gone.

'Will I be unlucky now?' asked Jeremy James.

'Not unless someone gives you a loaf of bread,' said Daddy.

They walked back across the square to say goodbye to the old lady, and now Jeremy James saw that she was not only covered with pigeons. She was also covered with 'Number Coo'.

'You must be very, very lucky,' said Jeremy James.

'Oh I am, sonny,' she said, 'I am. Look at all the friends I got, an' the nice people I meet. An' I'll tell yer somethin' else. 'Ave you ever bin on the Underground?'

'Yes,' said Jeremy James.

'An' yer've seen 'ow crowded it is?'

'Yes,' said Jeremy James.

'Well,' said the old lady. 'When I gets on, yer should see 'ow quick the carriage empties. Auntie Dot never 'as no trouble wi' crowds. Except o' course wi' crowds o' pigeons.'

CHAPTER FOUR

The Pry Monster

When they said goodbye to Auntie Dot, Daddy and Jeremy James walked down a broad street which was called Whitehall. Jeremy James wondered if it was called Whitehall because the pigeons had been there as well. In the middle of the street was a large white block which Daddy said was the Cenotaph, and was a monument to people who had been killed in the war.

'Is war a good thing?' asked Jeremy James.

'No,' said Daddy. 'It's very bad.'

'Did Nelson fight a war?'

'Yes, against the French.'

'Well, if war's a bad thing, why did they put Nelson on top of a pillar, if being on top of a pillar is a good thing?'

Daddy explained that war was bad, but winning a war was good. Jeremy James asked if winning a war was good for the people who had been killed, and Daddy said no, and it wasn't even good for the people who hadn't been killed.

'So who *is* it good for?' asked Jeremy James.

'Nobody really,' said Daddy, 'except soldiers and politicians.'

'Who's Polly Tishuns?' asked Jeremy James.

Daddy explained that politicians were people who told other people what to do, and pretended it was for their own good.

'Is Mummy a Polly Tishun?' asked Jeremy James.

'No,' said Daddy. 'When Mummy tells you to do something, it *is* for your own good. And when I tell you to do something, it's also for your own good. But when politicians tell you to do something, it's usually for *their* good.'

By now they had reached a narrow street which was closed off by a gate, and Daddy said this was Downing Street, where the Prime Minister lived. The Prime Minister was the bossiest politician of them all. Even the politicians who told everyone else what to do were themselves told what to do by the Prime Minister. And as a matter of fact, said Daddy, it was the Prime Minister who was ruining the country.

At that moment there was a buzz of excitement from all the people standing near the gate, and everybody moved back as it was opened. Through it came a group of smartly dressed people surrounded by a group of less smartly dressed people who were carrying cameras, microphones, notebooks and pencils.

'Look!' said Daddy. 'It's the Prime Minister!'

Suddenly the whole group stopped, right next to Daddy and Jeremy James, and the Prime Minister –

with a smile that came straight from the mouth –
leaned down and asked Jeremy James his name.

'Jeremy James,' said Jeremy James.

'And do you know who I am, Jeremy James?'
asked the Prime Minister.

'You're the Pry Monster,' said Jeremy James.

'Prime Minister,' said the Prime Minister. 'Good!
What a clever boy. And are you going to vote for me
at the next election, eh?'

Jeremy James didn't know what an election was,
but the look on the Prime Minister's face made it
clear that Jeremy James was supposed to say yes.

'No,' said Jeremy James.

The Prime Minister looked surprised.

'Oh? And may I ask why not?'

'Because,' said Jeremy James, 'you're ruining the
country.'

The Prime Minister looked even more surprised.
The smile disappeared from his face, and he glanced
at the people around him.

'Ahem!' he said. 'He obviously means *running* the
country.'

'No I don't,' said Jeremy James. 'You're a bossy
Polly Tishun.'

'Ha ha ha!' unlaughed the Prime Minister, glaring
at Daddy, who studied the top of Jeremy James's
head. 'Another little joke from the Opposition.' And
he walked quickly and stiffly away.

A man with a camera took a photograph of

Jeremy James, and another man with a notebook came up to him.

'Well done, young man!' he said. 'We'll have you on the front page tomorrow. "Jeremy James accuses Prime Minister of ruining the country".'

Everybody was smiling and nodding and congratulating Jeremy James. He wasn't quite sure what all the fuss was about, but he had a strange feeling that perhaps one day he might be put on top of a pillar, like Nelson, for having saved England.

CHAPTER FIVE

More Polly Tishuns

Further along the road, Daddy and Jeremy James came to a very grand and beautiful place called the Houses of Parliament, which was where Polly Tishuns met to tell one another what to do.

There was a small queue at one of the doors, and Daddy said they were lucky, because usually it was a large queue.

'I know why we're lucky,' said Jeremy James.

'Why?' asked Daddy.

'Because of the pigeon's "Number Coo",' said Jeremy James.

'Or "Number Queue",' said Daddy. 'Well, whatever it is, it's worked, because we're going in.'

At the entrance a man in uniform was searching people. When it came to Jeremy James's turn, the man looked very seriously at him, and asked if he had any guns or bombs. Jeremy James said he hadn't, but he'd like some if the man was giving them away.

'In this place,' said the man, 'you won't catch *anyone* giving anything away.'

Daddy and Jeremy James walked up stairs and along corridors, all of which were lined with statues and pictures, and then they suddenly found themselves on a sort of balcony. The balcony overlooked a very strange room: it was high and rather dark, and on both sides of a narrow gangway there were rows and rows of mainly empty green seats. A man in a funny wig was sitting at the far end of the room, and in the green seats were about thirty people, half of whom seemed to be asleep. Daddy and Jeremy James sat down to watch.

'It's all the Government's fault!' cried a thin man on one side of the room.

'Oh no it's not!' shouted a fat man on the other side.

'Oh yes it is!' cried the thin man.

'Order!' said the man in the wig. 'Order! Order!'

Jeremy James asked Daddy what was happening, and Daddy explained that this was called a debate. The Polly Tishuns were discussing what the Government had done, was doing, or was going to do: one side would say it was all very good, and the other side would say it was all very bad. At the end of the discussion, the Polly Tishuns would vote, and the side that said it was all very good would win.

'If they know who's going to win,' said Jeremy James, 'then why do they play?'

Daddy said it was all to do with some long word that Jeremy James didn't understand, and Jeremy James thought it was all to do with grown-ups doing silly things like sticking Nelson on a pillar.

Meanwhile, the debate continued:

'The Government,' said the thin man, 'is ruining the country.'

'Hear, hear!' said a bald man near him.

'Nonsense!' shouted the fat man. 'You'd ruin the country if you were in government.'

'Hear, hear!' said a hairy lady near him.

'No we wouldn't!' said the thin man.

'Yes you would!' said the fat man.

'Order!' said the man in the wig. 'Order! Order!'

'Since we are not in government,' continued the thin man, 'and since all the experts agree that the country is being ruined, and since the Government

claims that it is not responsible for ruining the country, then may I ask who is?'

'The Pry Monster!' shouted Jeremy James.

All heads turned, and there was loud laughter and applause from the people on the balcony and the people on the thin man's side of the room. Some of the people on the fat man's side woke up and didn't look very pleased. And on the balcony was a man in uniform who didn't look very pleased either. He started walking towards Jeremy James.

Daddy, with a rather red face, stood up.

'Come on, Jeremy James,' he said. 'Let's go and see the Queen instead.'

He took Jeremy James's hand just as the uniformed man arrived.

'Sorry about that,' said Daddy, 'but we were leaving anyway.'

Daddy and Jeremy James left the balcony, accompanied by the uniformed man and a round of loud applause.

'Sorry,' said Daddy again, when they were out in the corridor.

'That's all right, sir,' whispered the uniformed man. 'Made my day, that has.'

CHAPTER SIX

Seeing the Queen

'Does the Queen really live here?' asked Jeremy James.

'Yes,' said Daddy.

'It's as big as the Houses of Polly Mint.'

'Kings and queens always have big houses.'

'It must take her ages to hoover the carpet,' said Jeremy James.

They were standing outside Buckingham Palace, and Jeremy James gazed up at all the windows and wondered which one the Queen would look out of. Daddy said she might not look out of any of them, because she might not be there.

'If I had a house like that, I'd always be there,' said Jeremy James.

'So would I,' said Daddy. 'I'd never find my way out.'

'What do kings and queens *do*, Daddy?' asked Jeremy James.

'Well,' said Daddy, 'when they're not hoovering the carpet, they travel around meeting people. They open buildings, launch ships, and ride through the streets so that people can cheer them and wave their flags.'

'How do you become a king?'

'The best way is to get yourself a father who's a king. And make sure you haven't got any older brothers.'

'*I* haven't got any older brothers,' said Jeremy James.

'No,' said Daddy. 'But unfortunately, I'm not a king. Which I'm afraid means that you won't be a king either.'

This was a bit of a blow for Jeremy James. He rather liked the idea of being king. He could easily live in a big house like the Queen's, and he was good at meeting people, and he'd be very good at riding through the streets and being cheered. He wasn't sure how to open buildings or launch ships, but maybe somebody else could do that, and he would do some extra meeting people and being cheered.

'Can't *you* become a king, then, Daddy?' he asked.

Daddy shook his head.

'Well, could the Queen make *me* a king, then?' asked Jeremy James.

'You can ask her,' said Daddy, 'if you see her.'

The problem was how to see her. Even if she came to one of the windows, she'd be much too far away for Jeremy James to talk to. He'd need to go into the Palace itself. But when he told Daddy that he wanted to go into the Palace, Daddy said he'd never be allowed in, and it was time they were going anyway.

'They might let me in if I ask nicely,' said Jeremy James.

'I don't think so,' said Daddy, 'but you can try. There's a guard through the gate there. You can ask him, but if he says no, then we'll leave. Right?'

Jeremy James walked along the railings to a gate which was open, and standing inside the gate was a guard in a red uniform, with a high furry hat that came down over his eyes. He was standing very still, holding his gun like a walking stick, and staring straight ahead. Jeremy James went up to him.

'Excuse me,' he said.

The guard didn't move.

'Please can I go and see the Queen?'

Not a movement, not a word, not a blink. The guard was as stiff as a statue.

Suddenly Jeremy James began to laugh. Daddy had played another trick on him. This wasn't a real guard at all. He was a waxwork, like the models in Madame Tussaud's!

Jeremy James pulled the guard's tunic and poked his hand.

'If you don't go away, little boy,' said the guard out of the corner of his mouth, 'you'll get a thick ear.'

Jeremy James leapt back in amazement.

'I thought you were a waxwork,' he said.

'I may look like a waxwork,' said the guard, 'and

227

sometimes I feel like a waxwork, but I can give you a thick ear like no waxwork has ever given you.'

'I only want to see the Queen,' said Jeremy James.

'Well you can't,' said the guard. 'She's not at home.'

'Will she be back soon?' asked Jeremy James.

'Not till next Thursday,' said the guard. 'Can I give her a message?'

'Could you tell her that I want to be king?'

'Certainly, sir. And who shall I say was calling?'

'Jeremy James,' said Jeremy James.

'All right, Jeremy James, I'll inform Her Majesty,' said the guard. 'Now hop it before you get me into trouble.'

Jeremy James hopped back to Daddy, who was watching from the other side of the railings.

'Well, what did he say?' asked Daddy.

'He said he'd give me a thick ear,' said Jeremy James, 'and he'll tell the Queen I want to be king.'

'That's nice of him,' said Daddy. 'Or half nice of him.'

'But the Queen won't be back till Thursday,' said Jeremy James.

'That's bad luck,' said Daddy. 'We'll be gone by then.'

CHAPTER SEVEN

The Taxi Driver

It was time to leave Buckingham Palace anyway, because Daddy wanted to go to the hotel.

'We'll take a taxi,' he said, 'have a wash and a rest, and then get ready to see London by night. Agreed?'

Jeremy James agreed – except for the bit about a wash. That was another silly grown-up idea. When you got up, you had to have a wash. When you went out, you had to have a wash. When you came home, you had a wash, and when you went to bed you had a wash. Jeremy James reckoned that if he kept on washing whenever he was told to wash, pretty soon he'd finish up with no face left to wash. And then what would they do?

'Look, Mummy and Daddy,' he'd say. 'I haven't got any face.'

'Oh!' they'd say. 'Who are you?'

'Jeremy James,' he'd say.

'Well, Jeremy James,' they'd say, 'go and wash your blank space.'

Washing was a waste of soap, a waste of water, and a waste of face.

Jeremy James and Daddy stood by the roadside, and Daddy waved to a taxi, but the taxi took no notice. Another taxi came, Daddy waved again, and the second taxi took as much notice as the first taxi. A third and fourth taxi also went by, but when Jeremy James helped Daddy to wave at a fifth taxi, the people sitting in it waved back.

'They were nice,' said Jeremy James.

At last an empty taxi drew up beside them, and they climbed in.

'Hotel Jeremy, please,' said Daddy to the taxi driver, who was a thin man with glasses on his nose, stubble on his chin, and a flat cap on his head.

' 'Otel Jeremy?' repeated the taxi driver. 'Never 'eard of it.'

'It's in Jeremy Street,' said Daddy.

'Jeremy Street?' repeated the taxi driver. 'Never 'eard of it.'

'It's very near Welbeck Street,' said Daddy.

'Welbeck Street?' repeated the taxi driver. 'Where's that?'

'Um, well...' said Daddy.

'I wish you people'd pick places what I've 'eard of,' grumbled the taxi driver. 'I'm sick o' people goin' ter places I don't know. Makes my job very difficult.'

'Sorry,' said Daddy, 'but I thought that since you're a taxi driver...'

'Yeah,' said the taxi driver, 'ev'rybody finks that because yer a taxi driver yer must know everyfink. Where's this place? they ask. Where's that place? 'Ad someone this mornin' ask me the quickest way to 'Ighgate Cemetery. I told 'im the quickest way was ter jump under a bus. Now then...'

He pulled out a book, took off his glasses, muttered, 'Welbeck Street, Welbeck Street, Welbeck Street', and began to flick through the pages.

'Welbeck Street,' he said. 'Got it. Wot was the uvver street?'

'Jeremy Street,' said Daddy.

'Jeremy Street, Jeremy Street, Jeremy Street,' said the taxi driver. 'Jeremy Street. Got it. Is that where yer wanter go?'

'Yes, please,' said Daddy.

'Couldn't 'ave picked a much smaller street, could yer? No wonder I've never 'eard of it.'

They set off through the streets of London, and as the taxi dodged in and out of the traffic, the driver kept telling Daddy what terrible drivers all the other drivers were. Daddy said it must be a really difficult job, and the taxi driver said he'd only been doing it for three days, and if the next three days were as bad as the first three days, he wouldn't be doing it for much longer.

'London,' he said, 'is full o' people 'oo don't know where they're goin, an' drivers 'oo don't know wot they're doin'.'

'Daddy never knows where he's going,' said Jeremy James.

'I do know where I'm going,' said Daddy. 'I just don't know how to get there.'

'I got the same problem,' said the taxi driver. 'I dunno 'ow I managed ter pass me taxi-drivin' test, 'cos I ain't got no sense o' direction.'

Daddy asked him what he'd been doing before he became a taxi driver.

'I was a tourist guide,' he said. 'I only 'ad *that* job fer three days an' all. Took a party o' tourists to 'Ampton Court an' lost 'em in the maze.'

Jeremy James asked Daddy what a maze was, and he explained that it was a lot of paths that led into a place you couldn't get out of. Jeremy James asked if London was a maze, and Daddy said it was worse

233

than a maze because it was just as difficult to get in as to get out.

'Not ter mention gettin' 'round,' said the taxi driver, pulling in to the kerb. 'I'm lost.'

He pulled out his book.

'Now, where was it yer wanted ter go?' he asked.

'Daddy!' said Jeremy James. 'Isn't that our car park over there?'

'So it is!' said Daddy.

'Ah!' said the driver. 'Found it, 'ave I?'

'Pretty nearly,' said Daddy. 'This'll do, anyway.'

'Well fancy that!' said the driver. 'Must be my lucky day!'

Daddy and Jeremy James got out, and Daddy paid before they said goodbye to the driver and set off towards the car park. When Jeremy James looked back, the taxi was still there, and the taxi driver had taken off his glasses and was looking at his book.

'Do you think he'll find his way home?' asked Jeremy James.

'No,' said Daddy. 'And do you think we'll find our way to the hotel?'

'No,' said Jeremy James.

But before they didn't find their way to the hotel, Daddy wanted to fetch the cases from the car, and that meant finding the car. This might not have been quite so difficult if Daddy had remembered which floor it was on. Jeremy James remembered that it was in a space between two other cars, but for a long time they couldn't find the space or the other

two cars. And when at last they did find it, Jeremy
James realized that the space had been filled. Daddy's
car was in it.

They took out their bags, and then Daddy asked
the car park attendant the way to Jeremy Street.
Fortunately, it was only two minutes' walk away, and
so in exactly ten minutes (after Daddy had turned
left instead of right) they found themselves outside a
tall dark building with a big sign over the door that
read: HOTEL JEREMY.

CHAPTER EIGHT

The Bushy Man

Daddy and Jeremy James walked into the hotel. In the hallway a man was sitting at a table with his head in his hands and a bottle and glass next to his right arm.

'Good afternoon,' said Daddy.

The man raised his head, and Jeremy James found himself staring up at a square-shaped face with a bushy moustache and two bushy eyebrows. The two eyebrows were so bushy that at first Jeremy James thought the man had three moustaches.

'What a life!' said the man.

'It's not that bad, is it?' asked Daddy.

'Maybe yours isn't,' said the man. 'Business is terrible.'

'Oh dear,' said Daddy.

'I can't pay my mortgage.'

'Oh dear.'

'The chambermaid left last week.'

'Oh dear, oh dear.'

'And my wife left this morning.'

'Oh dear, oh dear, oh dear.'

'What a life!'

The bushy man poured some drink out of the bottle into the glass, and swallowed it with one gulp.

'I suppose you want a room,' he said.

Daddy explained that he'd already reserved a room by telephone, and the man looked in a book, said 'Ah!', stood up and sat down.

'Room thirty-three,' he said, 'third floor. Key's over there. I'd get it for you, but I'm having difficulty standing up.'

Daddy went behind the table and took a key down from a board that was full of keys.

'Lift's not working,' said the man. 'Nothing works in this hotel, including me. What a life!'

Daddy and Jeremy James made their way to the stairs.

'People aren't very happy in London, are they?' said Jeremy James to Daddy as he stomped upwards.

'Some of them are,' puffed Daddy.

'Well the bushy man isn't,' said Jeremy James. 'And the taxi man wasn't, and the Pry Monster wasn't, and the Polly Tishuns weren't.'

'The pigeon woman was happy,' panted Daddy. 'And we're happy, aren't we?'

'Yes,' said Jeremy James. 'I'm always happy.'

'So there are some happy people in London,' gasped Daddy. 'Though I shall be a lot happier when we've reached the third floor.'

Room 33 was at the end of the corridor. It was

a small room with two beds, a chair and a table, a wardrobe, a wash basin, and ... a telephone.

'Ah!' said Daddy. 'I'll tell you what we'll do. We'll have a wash, and then we'll phone Mummy, shall we?'

'You have a wash, Daddy,' said Jeremy James, 'and I'll phone Mummy.'

Daddy said they should both have a wash, and both phone Mummy. Jeremy James pointed out that he'd already had a wash in the fountain, but Daddy pointed out that they hadn't had any soap. Jeremy James noticed that there wasn't any soap in the wash basin, but Daddy took a small packet out of his bag. Jeremy James thought that was a piece of bad luck, but Daddy said it was a piece of soap.

When they'd finished washing, Daddy lifted Jeremy James up on to the table beside the telephone, so that they could ring Mummy.

'Would you like to press the numbers?' asked Daddy.

'Yes, please,' said Jeremy James.

Daddy took Jeremy James's hand and pressed his forefinger on the number 0. But before he could press another number, there was a ringing tone.

'What a life!' said a voice at the other end.

'Oh!' said Daddy. 'Is that reception?'

'Of course it's reception,' said the voice. 'What were you expecting, Buckingham Palace?'

'Sorry,' said Daddy, 'but I wanted to ring home.'

'Dial nine for an outside line,' said the voice. 'You might not get it, but it's worth a try.'

Daddy put the phone down, picked it up again, and pressed Jeremy James's finger on to the number 9. There were a few clicks, and then a humming noise.

'We're in luck,' said Daddy.

Jeremy James liked the telephone. It was a funny feeling talking to someone who wasn't there but whose voice came right into your ear. Once, when he'd been alone in the living room, he'd dialled a number and talked to a lady who lived hundreds of miles away. She'd even sent him a present afterwards. Jeremy James thought it was wonderful. Daddy thought it was expensive, and Jeremy James had been forbidden to do any more dialling.

It was Mummy who answered the phone, and when Daddy had said hello, he let Jeremy James talk to her.

'Hello,' said Jeremy James.

'Hello, Jeremy James,' said Mummy. 'Are you enjoying London?'

'Yes,' said Jeremy James. 'Everybody's unhappy except Daddy and me.'

'What are they unhappy about?' asked Mummy.

Jeremy James told Mummy all about the bushy Mr What-a-Life, the taxi driver who couldn't find the way, the Pry Monster who was ruining the country . . .

'And a pigeon did a Number Coo on my head,' said Jeremy James.

'Was the pigeon unhappy, too?' asked Mummy.

'Yes,' said Jeremy James, 'because he must have had a tummy ache.'

Jennifer was next on the phone.

'Hello, Jeffer,' said Jeremy James.

'Jem Jem!' said a delighted voice. 'Jem Jem gone Londy.'

'London,' said Jeremy James. 'Are you being a good girl?'

'No,' said Jennifer. 'Jeffer nor-ty.'

'You always are,' said Jeremy James.

Mummy also passed the phone to Christopher. Jeremy James said, 'Hello, Kwiffer,' but Kwiffer didn't say anything. Mummy told him to say something, but he still didn't say anything, and so Mummy asked to talk to Daddy.

After everybody had talked to everybody (except Kwiffer, who wouldn't talk to anybody), Daddy finally put the phone down.

'I like telephones,' said Jeremy James. 'When I grow up, I'm going to telephone a lot.'

'Well when you grow up,' said Daddy, 'just remember – if you want to say a lot, you're going to have to pay a lot.'

That was another grown-up idea: if you wanted something nice, you always had to pay for it. Nasties were free. You could have as many washes as you liked, and you wouldn't have to pay a penny.

'When I'm king,' said Jeremy James, 'nobody will have to pay for telephones.'

And secretly he added that when he was king, soap would cost a fortune.

CHAPTER NINE

An Amazing Meal

After a little rest, Daddy and Jeremy James were ready to see London by night.

'Off to enjoy yourselves, are you?' said the bushy man at the table.

'Yes,' said Jeremy James. 'We're going to be happy.'

'Lucky you,' said the man.

'What are *you* going to do?' asked Jeremy James.

'I'm going to stay here,' said the man, 'and be miserable.'

'You won't be happy if you're mizzable,' said Jeremy James.

'The way I feel,' said the man, 'I wouldn't even be happy if I was happy. What a life!'

It was dark outside now. Soon Daddy and Jeremy James were walking along a street full of brightly lit shops, red double-decker buses, black box-like taxis, hundreds of cars, and thousands of people. This road suddenly broadened out into a roundish area with streets going off at all angles, and huge flashing signs that kept changing their appearance.

'This is Piccadilly Circus,' said Daddy.

'I can't see any circus,' said Jeremy James.

'There isn't one,' said Daddy. 'That's just its name.'

'They shouldn't call it a circus if it isn't a circus,' said Jeremy James. 'That's cheating.'

They walked up one of the streets that led off Piccadilly Uncircus, and it had a lot of theatres in it.

'Would you like to go to the theatre tonight?' asked Daddy.

'Yes, please,' said Jeremy James.

'Right,' said Daddy, 'let's see if we can get two tickets.'

The theatre they went to had a lot of pictures of wolves outside, and Daddy said there was a musical show called *Wolfie* here, which he thought Jeremy James might enjoy. And when he'd bought the tickets, he had another suggestion: 'How about something to eat before the show?'

Daddy was full of good ideas this evening. He even knew which restaurant they would go to, *and* where it was. You had to go along the street, turn right here, and left here, and . . . no, wait a minute, back we go . . . it should have been right here, and left here, and . . . back we go . . . ah! There it is! The restaurant was called Le Campanile which Daddy said was French for bell tower, though it hadn't got a bell and it wasn't in a tower.

They were welcomed by a tiny bald man in a black jacket and bow tie.

'Bonsoir, messieurs,' he said. 'You veesh to ev a table for two personnes? Bon, come zees way, pleeze.'

He took them to a table in the corner, fetched a high cushion for Jeremy James, bowed his head to them both, and then with a flourish of his hand produced a menu.

Daddy read through the list, and Jeremy James chose chicken and chips, but Daddy said he'd had chicken and chips for lunch, and wouldn't he like to try something else? Like veal escalope, for instance? Jeremy James had never heard of Willy's gallop, but it did sound quite interesting, and since it came with chips, he said yes, all right.

Willy's gallop proved to be a success: thin slices of meat covered in golden batter, very tender, very tasty. And the chips were just as golden, crisp and crunchy.

'You don't want any dessert after that, do you, Jeremy James?' asked Daddy, when the last golden crumb had disappeared.

'Yes I do!' said Jeremy James.

A meal without a dessert was like Nelson's Column without Nelson.

'Right,' said Daddy. 'Follow me.'

Jeremy James followed Daddy across the restaurant to a large lighted cabinet. On the open shelves of the cabinet stood dish upon dish of puddings, pies, mousses, gâteaux, trifles, tarts, jellies, fruit salads, ice cream . . .

'Help yourself,' said Daddy.

Jeremy James's eyes opened as wide as two dessert bowls.

'To anything?' he asked.

'Whatever you like,' said Daddy.

'As much as I like?' asked Jeremy James.

'As much as you can get in the bowl,' said Daddy.

No dessert bowl was ever piled as high as Jeremy James's. He took a portion of pudding, a piece of pie, a mountain of mousse, a tremble of trifle, a tingle of tart, a judder of jelly, and an iceberg of ice cream. Heads turned to look at the amazing dessert bowl with legs as it made its way carefully across the restaurant to the table in the corner.

'You'll never be able to eat all that,' said Daddy, though his own bowl was almost as high as Jeremy James's.

'Nor will you,' said Jeremy James.

They were both wrong.

For the next ten minutes not a word was spoken, as spoons and forks scooped and sliced and squelched their way through the multi-coloured mouthfuls. If every Londoner could come and have dinner in the bell tower, thought Jeremy James, they would never be unhappy again.

When at last the bowl was empty, and Jeremy James was full, the little bald man in the black jacket and bow tie came to the table.

'Deed you enjoy ze meal?' he asked.

'Yes, thank you,' said Jeremy James. 'It was the best meal I've ever had.'

'Ah bon!' said the man. 'Zen per'eps you weel come again.'

'Yes, please,' said Jeremy James. 'When?'

'Whenevair you like,' said the man.

'Can we come tomorrow?' asked Jeremy James.

'You must ask your fazair,' said the man.

Jeremy James didn't know what a fazair was, but Daddy seemed to understand.

'We'll see you next time we're in London,' he said to the man.

'We're going to be in London tomorrow,' said Jeremy James.

Daddy had obviously forgotten that.

CHAPTER TEN

Wolf Watching

There were hundreds of people at the theatre, and unlike the Pry Monster, the taxi driver and the bushy man, they all seemed very happy. Maybe they'd been eating in bell towers as well.

Daddy and Jeremy James went up a broad staircase, Daddy showed his tickets to a smiling man at the door, and then they went inside a huge room that was full of purple seats. There was a purple curtain at one end of the theatre, and glass lamps hanging from the ceiling, and galleries and balconies and gold ornaments on all sides. Most of the seats were already sat in, and people were laughing and chattering, and Jeremy James noticed one lady with a box of chocolates in her hand. But even if she'd offered him one, he couldn't have eaten it. Not yet, anyway.

Jeremy James had been to theatres before. Once Daddy had had to talk to somebody, and Jeremy James had wandered on to the stage and had a chat with some of the actors. They hadn't been too pleased to see him, and one of them had carried him off the stage. The audience had liked seeing him, though, because they'd laughed and applauded. They'd also applauded on another occasion, when he and Daddy had gone on the stage with a magician named Marvello, who had smashed Daddy's watch, but hadn't really. Theatres were exciting places, and Jeremy James wondered if he'd be able to go up on this stage as well.

Daddy said excuse me to some people, who stood up and let them through to their seats. Jeremy James found himself sitting next to a lady with grey hair and a lot of sparkles round her neck.

'Hello,' said the lady.

'Hello,' said Jeremy James.

'What's your name?' she asked.

'Jeremy James,' said Jeremy James.

'And is this the first time you've been to the theatre, Jeremy James?' asked the lady.

'No,' said Jeremy James. 'I've been lots of times.'

At this moment, a tall man with a lot of hair sat right in front of Jeremy James.

'Can you see all right?' asked Daddy.

'Yes,' said Jeremy James. 'I can see a lot of hair.'

'Oh dear,' said Daddy. 'Here, try my seat.'

Daddy and Jeremy James changed places, but next to the tall man was a tall lady, and she had even more hair than the tall man.

'Can you see now?' asked Daddy.

'Yes,' said Jeremy James. 'I can see a lot more hair.'

The tall lady must have heard what Jeremy James had said, because she turned round in her seat.

'We're blocking your view, are we?' she said.

'The problem is,' said the sparkling lady with grey hair, 'that wherever Jeremy James sits, there'll be someone in front of him.'

'There's no one in front of us,' said the tall man, turning round. 'Let's all change places.'

'That's very kind of you,' said Daddy.

The tall man and the tall lady stood up, and then everybody in their row stood up to let them pass. And Daddy and Jeremy James also stood up, and everybody in their row stood up to let them pass as well. And just as the two rows were standing up, all the lights went out.

Jeremy James could see nothing in the sudden darkness, but he heard someone say 'Ouch!', and Daddy say 'Sorry!'

Jeremy James had just reached the end of the row when the lights went on again, the purple curtain swept open, and standing on the stage was a man dressed exactly like the little bald waiter in the bell tower.

'Are you all sitting comfortably?' he asked.

'No!' said Jeremy James.

A few people laughed.

'Sh!' said Daddy, excusing himself past the people in the next row.

'Good!' said the man. 'Then we can begin.'

'Not yet!' said Jeremy James.

A lot of people laughed.

'Jeremy James!' hissed Daddy. 'Sh!'

'But—'

'Sh!'

'Once upon a time,' said the man, 'in a deep dark forest, there lived a big bad wolf . . .'

Jeremy James sat down on his seat just as the big bad wolf came on to the stage, but Jeremy James could see straight away that it wasn't a wolf at all – it was a man dressed up as a wolf.

'I'm not a big bad wolf,' said the wolf.

'No, he's not,' said Jeremy James to Daddy. 'He's a man.'

'Sh!' said Daddy.

'I haven't had a decent meal in weeks,' said the wolf man, 'so I'm certainly not big. And what's bad about me? I'm one of the nicest wolves I know. So I'm not a big bad wolf at all. I'm a skinny nice wolf.'

From somewhere that Jeremy James couldn't see, an orchestra began to play, and the big bad skinny nice wolf man began to sing:

'Wolfie is my name,
Survival is my game,
I haven't had a bite in weeks,
Oh isn't it a shame!

Skinny as a feather,
I'm a piece of walking leather,
If I don't get my dinner soon,
I'll vanish altogether.'

On normal days, Jeremy James would have had a lot of sympathy for Wolfie, but tonight he didn't feel at all hungry.

'Red Riding Hood
Will be coming through the wood
With a basket full of goodies which I'd
Borrow if I could.'

It was when Wolfie mentioned the basket of goodies that Jeremy James suddenly felt a sharp pain in his tummy.

'Tender chicken breast,
Salad nicely dressed,
Cherry pie and ice cream,
A bottle of the best.'

'Daddy,' said Jeremy James.
'What is it?' whispered Daddy.
'I'm going to be sick,' said Jeremy James.
'What, now?' asked Daddy.
'Yes,' said Jeremy James.
'Hold on!' said Daddy.
He stood up, lifted Jeremy James from under the arms, and the whole row of people rose like a line of dominoes in reverse.
'Excuse me, sorry, excuse me, sorry...' said Daddy.

'Pickles in a jar,
Pot of caviar,
Half a pound of fudge cake,
And a chocolate bar.'

Daddy was racing up the aisle with Jeremy James over his shoulder and the nasty pain was getting nastier, and any second now . . .

Bang! Daddy had pushed open the door to the lavatory. Jeremy James leaned over, and out came a mixture of ice cream, jelly, tart, trifle, mousse, pie, pudding, chips and Willy's gallop.

'I shouldn't have let you eat so much,' said Daddy. 'No tummy in the world could have held on to all that dessert.'

Jeremy James had been sick once before. He'd eaten a whole box of liquorice allsorts, and Dr Bassett had come to the house to examine him. But Dr Bassett had said that Jeremy James had something called 'a touch of flu'.

'It wasn't the dessert, Daddy,' said Jeremy James. 'I've got a touch of flu.'

Daddy felt Jeremy James's forehead.

'Do you feel hot?' he asked.

'No,' said Jeremy James.

'Do you feel cold?' asked Daddy.

'No,' said Jeremy James.

'Do you feel like eating a bowlful of chocolate mousse, pie and ice cream?' asked Daddy.

Jeremy James thought for a moment.

'Not just yet,' he said.

'It's not a touch of flu,' said Daddy. 'It's a touch of over-eating.'

Then Daddy asked Jeremy James if he was feeling better, and Jeremy James said yes, and could they go back and watch the skinny nice wolf man again? But Daddy decided that they should go back to the hotel now because it was rather late, and actually he had a little bit of a pain in the tummy himself.

'Is over-eating catching, Daddy?' asked Jeremy James.

'It certainly is,' said Daddy.

As they left the theatre, the skinny nice wolf man

had just made his way to Granny's house, and the man in the black jacket and bow tie was telling the audience that Granny was sick. Maybe she had a touch of over-eating, too.

CHAPTER ELEVEN

Ampuluses

When Daddy and Jeremy James got back to the hotel, the bushy man was still sitting at his table, and his bottle was almost empty.

'Did you . . . hic . . . have a good time?' he asked.

'Yes, thank you,' said Jeremy James. 'I've been sick.'

'Sho have I,' said the man.

'I had a touch of over-eating,' said Jeremy James.

'That'sh funny,' said the man. 'I had a touch of over-drinkin'. Shame thing, more or lesh. What a life!'

Daddy and Jeremy James left him sitting there. Daddy was in quite a hurry to go upstairs, because the pain in his tummy had got worse, and so as soon as they'd gone into Room 33, he went out again.

Jeremy James sat on the bed and looked round the room. There wasn't very much to look at. There wasn't very much to do, either. He bounced on the bed a couple of times, and then went across to Daddy's bed and bounced on that, but the beds

256

weren't very bouncy, and in any case bouncing on beds wasn't all that interesting.

The wardrobe wasn't interesting either. There was nothing in it except dust. The ceiling was boring, the walls were boring, the brown curtains were boring, the wash basin was very boring, the chair was boring, the table was boring . . . except that on the table was the telephone. The telephone wasn't boring. No, the telephone was really interesting.

Jeremy James wandered across to the table and looked at the telephone. Ever since he'd spoken to the lady hundreds of miles away, he'd been forbidden to do any dialling. But that was at home. This telephone wasn't at home. This telephone was in the hotel. Daddy wouldn't have to pay the bill for the telephone in the hotel, would he?

Jeremy James climbed up on to the chair, so that he could have a closer look at the telephone. It was a nice telephone. Brown, like the curtains. And with numbers. There, for instance, was the 0 that Daddy had got him to press before he'd spoken to the bushy man.

Jeremy James wondered if someone might already be talking on the telephone. There was certainly no harm in just picking it up and listening. And so he picked up the receiver. There was a humming noise.

If he were to press the 0, the bushy man would say: 'What a life!' It wouldn't be much fun talking to the bushy man. If you wanted to talk to somebody else, you had to press 9. That was how you got really interesting conversations.

Jeremy James pressed the 9. The humming sound stopped, but nothing else happened, and so he pressed 9 again. There was a click, but that was all. He pressed again. Another click. Once more, thought Jeremy James, and pressed the 9 again.

There was a very short *brrr*, and then a woman's voice said: 'What service do you want? Police, fire or ambulance?'

This was a bit of a surprise for Jeremy James, because he hadn't realized that he wanted any service, and now he had a choice of three.

'What service do you want, caller?' asked the woman again. 'Police, fire or ambulance?'

'Police,' he said. They'd be the most fun to talk to.

'What is your name, caller?' asked the woman.

That was an easy question.

'Jeremy James,' said Jeremy James.

'Telephone number?'

That wasn't such an easy question. Jeremy James didn't know.

'Can you give me your telephone number?' asked the woman.

That was an easy question again.

'No,' said Jeremy James.

'Where are you, Jeremy James?'

Another easy question.

'Hotel Jeremy,' he said.

There were some clicks, and then a man's voice came on the line.

'Police,' said the man.

'Hello, police,' said Jeremy James.

'What's the trouble, son?' asked the man.

This was one of the difficult questions. Jeremy James didn't know of any trouble. And so he didn't answer.

'I understand you're in a hotel, is that right?' said the man.

'Yes,' said Jeremy James.

'Who's with you?'

'Nobody.'

'You're all alone?'

'Yes.'

There was a slight pause, and then the man asked where Mummy was. Jeremy James told him that she was at home. Next he asked where Daddy was, and Jeremy James started to say that he'd gone . . . well, he was going to tell the man that Daddy had gone to the lavatory, but grown-ups don't like talking about lavatories, and so Jeremy James simply said, 'He's gone', and left it at that.

'Gone?' echoed the policeman.

'He had a pain,' explained Jeremy James.

'He had a pain and he's gone?' cried the policeman.

Then Jeremy James heard him say to someone: 'Ring for an ambulance, quick!' Next the policeman asked Jeremy James if he knew the number of the room he was in, and Jeremy James told him it was 33.

'Stay right there, Jeremy James,' said the policeman. 'We'll be with you in a minute.'

The telephone went very quiet, and so Jeremy James put it down. It was very kind of the policeman to say he'd come, and that would certainly be a nice surprise for Daddy. But it seemed a bit silly to ring for an ambulance as well, because they'd never be able to get an ambulance up the stairs to Room 33. Unless perhaps the policeman was going to take Jeremy James downstairs to look at the ambulance. Jeremy James wondered what exactly ambulances were for. He'd seen them in the street – they were big and white, and sometimes flashed their lights and made loud pah-pah noises, but what did people do in them?

Daddy came into the room. He was a little pale.

'Daddy, what are ampuluses for?' asked Jeremy James.

Daddy stretched out on his bed.

'What are what for?' he asked.

'Ampuluses.'

'What are ampuluses?' asked Daddy.

'Big white cars that flash their lights and go pah-pah,' said Jeremy James.

'Oh, ambulances,' said Daddy. 'They take sick people to hospital. What made you ask . . .?'

At that very moment, there were loud pah-pah

noises from the street, and they seemed to come right outside the hotel before they stopped.

'Well, I'm blowed!' said Daddy. 'What a coincidence! That sounds like an ambulance arriving at the hotel. Unless it's the police. Fancy that! Just when you were asking about them!'

Daddy was even more surprised when half a minute later there was a knock on the door, and in came one policeman, one policewoman, and two men carrying a stretcher.

'Oh!' said Daddy.

'Ah!' said the policeman.

'Hello,' said Jeremy James.

'You must be Jeremy James,' said the policeman.

'Yes,' said Jeremy James.

'And are you his father, sir?' the policeman asked Daddy.

'Yes, of course I am,' said Daddy.

'And you're not dead, sir?'

'No, not as far as I know.'

'Dying, perhaps, sir?'

'No.'

'Slightly ill, maybe?'

'Well,' said Daddy, 'I did have a bit of an upset stomach. Do you mind telling me what this is all about?'

'Excuse me,' said one of the men with the stretcher, 'but do you need an ambulance or don't you?'

'It doesn't look as if we do,' said the policeman.

'Then we'll be on our way,' said the stretcher man.

The two men with the stretcher left, and the policeman took out a notebook and wrote something down
in it.

'I wish you'd tell me what's going on,' said Daddy.

'I think, sir,' said the policeman, 'that maybe your
son should tell us *all* what's going on.'

Jeremy James began to have a strange feeling that
whatever was going on should not have been going
on. The policeman certainly hadn't come to play
games or to show him what ampuluses were for, and
if he were to ask now what the trouble was, Jeremy
James would be able to tell him. The trouble was
what Jeremy James was in. Daddy was looking at
him, the policeman was looking at him, and the
policewoman was looking at him, and the look with
which they were looking at him had an almost magical effect on his eyes. One moment they were completely dry, and the next they were full of tears, which
at once started to trickle down his face. And the
magic spread to his bottom lip, which began to go
all wiggly . . .

'It's all right,' said the policewoman, kneeling down
beside him. 'There's no need to cry.'

Jeremy James thought there was every need to
cry. It was not only that he actually felt like crying,
but also it seemed to him that the more he cried, the
less he'd have to explain.

'I know what happened,' said the policewoman.
'Your Daddy had a pain, didn't he?'

Jeremy James nodded tearfully.

'And then he went out and left you alone. Is that right?'

Jeremy James nodded tearfully.

'And when he didn't come back, you thought something terrible had happened, didn't you?'

Jeremy James hadn't thought any such thing, but he was getting into the swing of things now, so he nodded tearfully.

'And then you rang nine-nine-nine to get some help for him.'

Jeremy James nodded tearfully.

The policewoman stood up and rested her hand on Jeremy James's shoulder.

'I think,' she said, 'that Jeremy James is a very clever boy. He thought his Daddy was dying, and he wanted to save him. Isn't that right, Jeremy James?'

Jeremy James nodded not quite so tearfully. He liked having the policewoman's hand on his shoulder. Somehow it made him feel that even if he was in trouble, trouble couldn't get to him.

'That sounds very possible,' said the policeman, who then looked rather severely at Daddy. 'But if that's true, sir, you shouldn't have left the little boy on his own.'

'Well, officer,' said Daddy, 'where I was going, I could hardly have taken him with me.'

'Anyway, I'm glad you're not as "gone" as we thought you were, sir. And as for you, young man,' said the policeman looking down at Jeremy James, who looked up at the policeman, 'we could do with bright lads like you in the police force, so if you ever need a job, come and see us.'

Jeremy James's eyes dried as magically as they had moistened.

'Yes, please!' he said. 'I *would* like a job!'

'Well, not just yet,' said the policeman. 'You'd better grow up first, or the helmet won't fit you.'

Then the policeman and policewoman said good-bye to Daddy and Jeremy James, and the police-woman gave Jeremy James a kiss, so he gave her a big kiss in return. She'd earned it.

'You didn't really think anything had happened to me, did you?' said Daddy when they'd gone.

Jeremy James looked at the floor.

'You were playing with the telephone, weren't you?'

Jeremy James wished he had the policewoman's hand on his shoulder again.

'And what have you been told about telephones?'

'I mustn't play with them,' said Jeremy James, still studying the carpet.

'Lucky for you that you had such a good lawyer,' said Daddy, 'or we'd really have been in trouble. Now, do you promise never to play with telephones again?'

'I promise,' said Jeremy James.

'Right,' said Daddy. 'Then let's have a wash and go to bed.'

Jeremy James would have liked to say, 'Oh no, not another wash!' But instead, he said, 'Yes, Daddy.'

When he'd had his wash and brushed his teeth, Daddy tucked him up in bed and turned the light out.

All the same, thought Jeremy James, as he lay there in the darkness, something *might* have happened to Daddy, and if something *had* happened to Daddy, he'd have been pleased that Jeremy James had dialled 999. And the policewoman would have been right to say how clever Jeremy James was.

'The policewoman was the nicest person in London, wasn't she, Daddy?' said Jeremy James.

But Daddy was fast asleep. He'd had a very tiring day.

CHAPTER TWELVE

Breakfast

Jeremy James was looking forward to breakfast. He and Daddy went downstairs to the breakfast room, where there were about a dozen tables, most of which had one or two grey-suited men sitting at them. Daddy and Jeremy James sat in a corner and waited.

After a few minutes, a thin, long-faced woman with wispy brown hair and a white apron came in carrying a tray, which she put in front of a fat, bald-headed man at the next table. Then she turned to Daddy and Jeremy James.

'What do you want for breakfast?' she asked.

'Egg and bacon,' said Jeremy James. 'Please.'

'You'll be lucky,' said the woman. 'Coffee or tea?'

Daddy said he'd have coffee, and Jeremy James would have orange juice, and the woman nodded and went away.

'Some funny goings-on here last night,' said the fat man at the next table.

'Oh?' said Daddy. 'What sort of goings-on?'

'The police were here, and an ambulance.'

'Really?' said Daddy.

'Yes,' said the man. 'Strange business. The owner got drunk and fell down the cellar steps. Only the police and ambulance hadn't come for him at all.'

'Hadn't they?' said Daddy.

'No,' said the fat man. 'Somebody else had sent for them, but that was a false alarm. Then just as the ambulance men were going out, they saw the cellar door open and heard somebody groaning. Poor chap had broken an arm *and* a leg. I came in when they were taking him out. Amazing stroke of luck that someone had just dialled nine-nine-nine.'

'It certainly was,' said Daddy.

'I dialled nine-nine-nine,' said Jeremy James.

'Did you?' asked the man.

'He did it by accident,' said Daddy.

'That's how the owner fell down the steps,' said the man. 'By accident. Broken arm and leg. What a life, eh?'

'I expect that's what he said, too,' remarked Daddy.

'The waitress is his wife,' whispered the fat man.

Daddy said he thought the owner's wife had left him, but the fat man said she'd come back when she heard about the accident.

'She hates this place,' he said. 'Can't blame her, either. Who'd want a job in a place like this with a man like that? Now he's going to be off for weeks, and she's stuck here till she can get someone to take over. That's why she's in such a vile mood.'

The long-faced woman came in with a tray, which she put down on the table in front of Daddy and Jeremy James. On it were a cup of coffee, a glass of orange juice, and four bread rolls with some butter and marmalade.

'Where's breakfast?' asked Jeremy James.

'That's it,' said the woman, and went away.

'It's what they call a Continental breakfast,' said Daddy.

'I don't want a conky mental breakfast,' said Jeremy James. 'I want a real breakfast.'

The fat man hadn't wanted a conky mental breakfast either, but apparently everybody had to have the same because it was the owner who always did the cooking, and now he was in hospital.

'You seem to know a lot about this hotel,' said Daddy.

'Oh I do,' said the fat man. 'And I'll tell you something else. My room hadn't been cleaned.'

'Ah, well,' said Daddy. 'I can tell *you* something about that. The chambermaid left last week.'

'I know,' said the fat man. 'No chambermaid ever stays in this place more than a few weeks. And frankly, one night's enough for me. But I shall feel really sorry for the owner when he comes out of hospital.'

'Why?' asked Daddy.

'Because he's going to find himself in even worse trouble,' said the fat man.

Daddy said that, considering the owner was in hospital with a broken arm and leg, his wife was going to leave him, the chambermaid *had* left him, he couldn't pay his mortgage, and the lift wasn't working, he might have difficulty finding any more trouble to get into.

'You'd be surprised,' said the fat man. 'Just when you've slid to the bottom of the hill, that's when the avalanche hits you.'

'What's his next bit of trouble, then?' asked Daddy.

'Me,' said the fat man. 'I'm a hotel inspector.'

CHAPTER THIRTEEN

Dinosaurs

Daddy and Jeremy James were to meet Mrs Robinson, the important lady, for lunch, and so Daddy said they would leave their bags in the car and spend the morning at the Natural History Museum.

After the breakfast-that-wasn't-a-breakfast, they packed their bags and went downstairs to pay the bill. The long-faced lady – now without her apron – was sitting at the table.

'We'd like to pay,' said Daddy.

'Not many people would,' said the lady.

She looked in a book, wrote something down on a piece of paper, gave it to Daddy, and Daddy gave her some money.

'How's your husband?' he asked.

'Plastered,' she said, 'one way or another. Was it your little boy that rang for the ambulance?'

'That's right,' said Daddy.

Jeremy James waited for her to say thank you, and what a clever boy, and here's your reward.

'With all that whisky in him,' she said, 'you should have sent for the fire brigade.'

Daddy and Jeremy James said goodbye to her, and set off for the car park.

'I think I know why London people are so unhappy,' said Jeremy James.

'Why?' asked Daddy.

'Because,' said Jeremy James, 'they don't eat a real breakfast.'

When they'd left their cases in the car, they went on the underground again, and from the underground station walked to the Natural History Museum. This turned out to be another palace, and as they walked through the door, Jeremy James found himself looking out for the Queen. But what he actually saw was a hundred times more eye-wide-opening than even the Queen. Standing ahead of him, in a vast hall, was the biggest animal he had ever seen.

To be more precise, it was the skeleton of the biggest animal he had ever seen. If it hadn't been an animal, it might have been a ship, it was so huge.

'What is it, Daddy?' gasped Jeremy James.

'It's a dinosaur,' said Daddy. 'It's called Diplodocus.'

'Dipperdopus!' said Jeremy James.

'It's one of the biggest animals that ever lived,' said Daddy.

They stepped into the hall, and gazed up at the mighty monster. The cage of its ribs could have held twenty lions, and you could have stood a church on the pillars of its legs. The tail was almost as long as the body, and stretched all the way down to the floor. As for the bones of the neck, they reached out like another tail that extended along the ceiling until it ended up in a surprisingly tiny head.

'Why has it got such a small head, Daddy?' asked Jeremy James.

'Because if its head was any bigger,' said Daddy, 'its neck would fall down.'

'I wish I was a Dipperdopus!' said Jeremy James.

'If you were,' said Daddy, 'I don't know what we'd give you for breakfast.'

'A thousand eggs and bacon,' said Jeremy James.

He asked Daddy if there were any Dipperdopuses wandering around London, but Daddy said the Dipperdopus had been dead for 150 million years.

'What did it die of?' asked Jeremy James.

'Overweight, I expect,' said Daddy.

When Jeremy James finally took his wide eyes off the Dipperdopus, they came to rest on a quite amazing head that was nearby. It was the sort of head any monster would be proud of. It was thick and heavy, with staring, glaring eyes and massive jaws that were open in a grin you might expect from the Devil. But what was truly terrifying was its teeth. They were as long and sharp and pointed as a row of daggers, and Jeremy James guessed that with a single crunch of those teeth, the monster could have cracked a thousand lollipops. With a head like that, it wouldn't need to kill its enemies – they'd die of fright just looking at it.

'Tyrannosaurus,' said Daddy. 'The fiercest of all the dinosaurs.'

'He ought to be in the Chamber of Horace,' said Jeremy James.

It was a pity Tyrannosaurus had lost his body, and Jeremy James wondered what had happened to it.

'He probably ate it,' said Daddy.

'If the Runny Roarus had a fight with the Dopey Dippus,' said Jeremy James, 'who would win?'

'Well, the Diplodocus might just possibly squash the Tyrannosaurus,' said Daddy, 'but my guess is that the Tyrannosaurus would eat the Diplodocus. And afterwards die of indigestion.'

Diplodocus and Tyrannosaurus weren't the only dinosaurs in the hall, and the dinosaurs weren't the only monsters in the museum. In another hall was the biggest animal in the world – a blue whale – and Daddy said there were still blue whales swimming in the sea today. But although the blue whale was as hugely huge as London, it didn't have the mighty legs of a Diplodocus, or the fearsome teeth of a Tyrannosaurus. And although Daddy took Jeremy James to other rooms that were full of birds, and creepy-crawlies, and human beings, none of them had Diplodocus legs or Tyrannosaurus teeth either. What Jeremy James really wanted to do was to go and have another look at the dinosaurs.

When they got back into the dinosaur hall, the first thing Jeremy James noticed was a smartly dressed lady with a feathery hat, and a ginger-headed boy with freckles. The lady was looking up at Diplodocus, and the ginger-headed boy was baring his teeth and snarling at Tyrannosaurus.

'Look, Daddy!' said Jeremy James. 'It's Timothy and Mrs Smy-Fossycoo!'

The Smyth-Fortescues lived next door. Timothy was a year older than Jeremy James, and he was believed to be the cleverest boy in the world – though he was the only person who believed it.

'Hello, Mrs Smyth-Fortescue. Hello, Timothy,' said Daddy. 'Fancy meeting you here.'

'Oh, what a coincidence!' said Mrs Smyth-Fortescue. 'We've just dropped Mr Smyth-Fortescue at the airport – one of his business trips, you know

– and I thought I'd bring dear Timothy here. He does so love the animals . . .'

While Mrs Smyth-Fortescue talked and Daddy listened, Jeremy James and Timothy wandered around the Diplodocus.

'I bet you don't know what it's called,' said Timothy.

'Yes I do,' replied Jeremy James. 'It's a Dippy Dopus.'

'No it's not,' said Timothy. 'It's a skelington.'

'It's not. It's a Dippy Dopus.'

'You don't know anything.'

'Yes I do. I know how long Dippy Dopus has been dead.'

'It's not a Dippy Dopus,' said Timothy. '*You're* a Dippy Dopus. That's a skelington, and how long has it been dead?'

'A million hundred and fifty years.'

'No, it hasn't.'

'Yes it has, because Daddy said so. Go and ask him.'

Timothy looked across to where Daddy and Mrs Smyth-Fortescue were chatting.

'Who cares?' he said. 'Nobody cares how long a skelington's been dead.'

Jeremy James cared. Because he knew that it *was* a Dippy Dopus, and it *did* die a million hundred and fifty years ago. And Timothy always pretended he knew everything, but he didn't.

'Well I know something else too,' said Jeremy James.

'What?' asked Timothy.

'Not telling,' said Jeremy James.

' 'Cos you don't know anything.'

'Yes I do.'

'Tell us then if you know, but you don't.'

'I know,' said Jeremy James, 'that Dippy Dopus is one of the biggest animals that ever lived.'

'No it's not.'

'Yes it is.'

'I've seen animals a lot bigger than that.'

'No you haven't.'

'Yes I have.'

'Where?'

Again Timothy looked across at Daddy and Mrs Smyth-Fortescue, and then he lowered his voice.

'In America,' he said. 'They've got animals ten times bigger than that in America.'

'They can't have,' said Jeremy James.

'Yes they have. In America everything's bigger than it is here. This skelington's small compared to the animals they've got in America. In America kids like you go for rides on little animals like this.'

'You couldn't ride a Dippy Dopus!' gasped Jeremy James.

'People ride them all the time in America,' said Timothy.

'*Nobody* could ride a Dippy Dopus!'

'It's easy.'

Jeremy James said it was impossible. Timothy said he'd ridden animals ten times bigger than the skelington, Jeremy James said Timothy couldn't even ride *this* skelington, and Timothy said yes he could, and just watch me.

Then he did something Jeremy James thought he ought not to have done. Around the Diplodocus was a sort of low glass wall, and Timothy suddenly clambered over the low glass wall and ran to the dinosaur's tail.

'Hey! Come back!' shouted an angry voice, but before the owner of the voice – a man with fiery eyes and a furry moustache – could stop him, Timothy was already climbing up the tail.

The fiery, furry man leapt over the low glass wall, and shouted: 'Get off of there right now!' But Timothy was out of his reach, and simply went on climbing.

'Oh dear!' said Mrs Smyth-Fortescue. 'It's my Timothy!'

'Oh dear!' said Daddy. 'So it is!'

Now everyone was looking at the ginger-headed boy making his way on all fours up the Diplodocus's tail. And as Timothy reached the top of the tail, he suddenly looked down and saw everybody looking up.

'What's he doing up there?' asked Daddy, who had come round to stand with Jeremy James.

'He said he could ride Dippy Dopus,' replied Jeremy James, 'and I said he couldn't.'

'It looks as if you were right,' said Daddy.

Timothy was now holding on to the bones round about where the dinosaur's bottom would have been if he'd had one, and Timothy's freckled face had turned rather white.

'Who does that child belong to?' shouted the fiery, furry man.

'Erm well, oh dear, he's mine!' said Mrs Smyth-Fortescue.

'Then tell him to come down!'

'Timothy, darling!' called Mrs Smyth-Fortescue. 'Come down now, please, there's a good boy!'

'I can't!' cried Timothy.

'Yes, you can, darling!' called Mrs Smyth-Fortescue.

'I'm stuck!' cried Timothy, and even from down below, Jeremy James could see the freckled face beginning to crumple.

'You'll be in trouble for this!' roared the fiery, furry man in the sort of voice you might expect from a Tyrannosaurus.

'Help!' howled Timothy – though it wasn't clear whether he needed help because he couldn't get down, or help because he was going to be in trouble.

At this moment anyway, help arrived, in the shape of two uniformed men carrying a ladder.

'Stay where you are, son!' called one of the men.

Timothy was in no state to do anything else.

The men placed the ladder against the leg of the Diplodocus, and then while one of them kept the

ladder steady, the other climbed up. There was a great cheer as he caught hold of Timothy, draped him over his shoulder, and climbed down again.

Timothy had closed his eyes very tight as the man had carried him down, but when they reached the floor, he opened them again and looked straight at Jeremy James.

'I told you you couldn't ride him,' said Jeremy James.

Mrs Smyth-Fortescue took Timothy from the arms of the man who had rescued him.

'There, there, darling!' she said. 'Are you all right?'

'The question, madam,' said the Tyrannosaurus man, 'is whether the dinosaur is all right. If not, it's going to cost you a packet. Now if you and your little darling would just follow me . . .'

'Oh dear,' said Mrs Smyth-Fortescue. 'I'm sure Timothy didn't mean any harm.'

She nodded goodbye to Daddy and Jeremy James, and Timothy lifted his head long enough to poke out his tongue at Jeremy James. Then they made their way through quite a large crowd of people – some of whom were laughing while others were shaking their heads – and disappeared through a door that was marked 'Private'.

'I know why Timothy couldn't ride it,' said Jeremy James.

'Why?' asked Daddy.

'Because,' said Jeremy James, 'he didn't know it was a Dippy Dopus. He thought it was a skelington.'

Daddy laughed and said that dinosaurs were not for riding anyway, and buses and trains were, and it was time they went for lunch with Mrs Robinson.

CHAPTER FOURTEEN

Mrs Robinson

Jeremy James had never seen so many books. Daddy's books at home were all over the place, but in Mrs Robinson's office there were books all over the books that were all over the place. There were shelves and piles and boxes and tablefuls of them. And in the middle of this one-room library was a desk, in front of which sat Daddy, with Jeremy James standing beside him, and behind which sat little Mrs Robinson. She had grey hair tied in a bun, a tiny turned-up nose, and very soft cheeks down which two thin lines of tears were trickling.

'I'm sorry, John,' she was saying, 'but I've got some awful news. I've been given the sack.'

Daddy said, 'Oh!' and looked very serious.

'I just don't know what I'm going to do,' said Mrs Robinson.

Jeremy James looked round the room, but he could see no sign of a sack. All he could see were books. Maybe the sack had got hidden under the books. What he couldn't understand, though, was why getting a sack should be so awful. Father Christmas

brought a sack round at Christmas time, and everybody was very pleased to see him. Jeremy James
would have liked a whole sack to himself.

'Daddy,' whispered Jeremy James, while Mrs Robinson wiped her eyes with her handkerchief. 'If Mrs
Robinson doesn't want it, can I have it?'

'Have what, Jeremy James?' asked Daddy.

'The sack,' said Jeremy James.

'Getting the sack,' said Daddy, 'means losing your
job.'

Mrs Robinson had heard the questions, and
laughed in spite of her tears.

'Sorry, Fiona,' said Daddy, 'but I suppose it is a
funny expression.'

'Did you think it was a sack of toys, Jeremy James?' asked Mrs Robinson.

'Yes,' said Jeremy James.

'I wish it was,' said Mrs Robinson. 'Then I'd give it to you with pleasure.'

She explained to Daddy that the company had been taken over by another company, and the new owners already had someone – a much younger person – to do her job, so they didn't need her any more. She'd been given a month's notice, and would be able to finish her work on Daddy's book, but then she'd have to find another job.

'And that won't be easy at my age,' she said.

Daddy said several times how sorry he was, and how he wished he could help her, and Jeremy James wished he could help her, too.

'Anyway,' said Mrs Robinson, 'it's lunchtime. Are you hungry, Jeremy James?'

Jeremy James was as hungry as a dinosaur, and as they left Mrs Robinson's office, he whispered to Daddy: 'Can we go to the bell tower?'

Daddy shook his head.

'Why not?' whispered Jeremy James.

'Because we're going somewhere else,' whispered Daddy.

The three of them walked down Welbeck Street, turned left, turned right, turned left again, and . . .

'Oh look!' cried Jeremy James. 'It's our hotel!'

Jeremy James was quite pleased to see the hotel again – until he remembered something . . .

'But they've only got rolls and marmalade!' he said.

'Don't worry, we're not going there for lunch,' said Mrs Robinson.

The place where they did go for lunch was full of gold dragons and lanterns and beautiful wiggly lamps. What it didn't seem to have was a cabinet full of mousses, puddings, pies, etc., and it turned out that they didn't have chicken and chips or Willy's gallop either. What they did have, though, was a delicious bowl of rice with all kinds of things in it. There were pieces of chicken, egg, various vegetables, shrimps, and green bits, red bits, and yellow bits. Each mouthful tasted different, and although it was a pity there weren't any chips, it was certainly the best meal Jeremy James had eaten since last night's dinner at Le Campanile.

Every so often during the meal, Jeremy James noticed Mrs Robinson wiping a tear from her eye, and his mind would wander from his bowl to her sack. If only he could find her a job, then she wouldn't have to be yet another of those unhappy London people – but how did people get jobs? The policeman had said that the police force needed bright lads, but Mrs Robinson wasn't a lad. Besides, he'd said that Jeremy James would have to grow up first or the helmet wouldn't fit him, and little Mrs Robinson certainly hadn't grown enough for the helmet to fit her.

The rice was followed by ice cream – several different flavours which helped to take Jeremy James's mind off the job again. But when the last mouthful had melted away, and the spoon had been licked clean, twice on both sides, Jeremy James suddenly had an idea. It came into his head almost as if someone had fed it to him. He could hardly wait for Daddy and Mrs Robinson to finish their conversation and their coffee.

At last the three of them stepped out into the street, and Jeremy James wished they could walk on the right side. If they didn't, it was going to be very difficult for him to get Mrs Robinson a job. He was lucky – or rather, Mrs Robinson was lucky. They *were* on the right side. He held on to Daddy's hand, and while Daddy talked to Mrs Robinson, Jeremy James waited and waited until the moment came.

'Hey! Jeremy James!' cried Daddy, as Jeremy James suddenly let go of his hand and raced away.

As they were on the right side, he didn't have to race far. With half a dozen steps, he was through the open door of Hotel Jeremy, and running along the hallway. As he ran, he wished very, very hard that the long-faced, wispy-haired woman would be sitting at the table where the bushy man had sat. It must have been wishes-come-true day, because there she was, as miserable as she'd been at breakfast.

'Forgotten something, have you?' she asked, as Jeremy James skidded to a halt in front of her.

'No,' said Jeremy James. 'Is the bushy man still in hospital?'

'My husband, you mean,' said the woman. 'Yes, of course he is.'

'And you don't want to do his job, do you?' said Jeremy James.

'No,' answered the woman.

'So can you give his job to Mrs Robinson?' asked Jeremy James.

At this moment, Daddy arrived.

'Please!' pleaded Jeremy James.

The long-faced woman looked from Jeremy James to Daddy and back to Jeremy James.

'Who's Mrs Robinson?' she asked.

'She's the lady with the sack,' said Jeremy James.

'What's going on?' asked Daddy.

'Well,' said the woman, 'your little boy's just asked me to give my job to Mrs Robinson, who's the lady with the sack.'

Daddy looked long and hard at Jeremy James, and suddenly burst out laughing. He quickly explained to the long-faced woman all about Mrs Robinson's sack, and then something quite extraordinary happened. The woman's long face became shorter and wider, and the droopy corners of her mouth began to go up instead of down, and her eyes – which had been as dull as rolls and marmalade – became as shiny as fried eggs. Then her lips opened, and out came a laugh even louder than Daddy's. Jeremy James had never seen a face change so quickly. It was like the sun coming out from behind a cloud.

288

'Come on, Jeremy James,' said Daddy. 'Poor Mrs Robinson'll be wondering what's happened.'

'But she hasn't got the job yet!' said Jeremy James. 'Please can she have the job? Please!'

The shorter-and-wider-faced woman reached across the table and ruffled Jeremy James's hair.

'Of course she can have it,' she said. 'But only if she wants it.'

'Thank you!' cried Jeremy James, and danced out of Hotel Jeremy, leaving the woman sitting back in her chair, shaking her head and smiling.

But Mrs Robinson didn't want the job. She had a little cry when Daddy told her what had happened, and Daddy had to explain to Jeremy James that Mrs Robinson wanted to do book work and not hotel work.

'She could put all her books in the hotel!' said Jeremy James. 'She'd have more room for them there!'

'That's true,' said Daddy, 'but she wouldn't have time to read them.'

Mrs Robinson had dried her eyes, and crouched down beside Jeremy James.

'Thank you very, very much, Jeremy James,' she said. 'I'll never forget what you've just done for me. And I feel a lot better knowing there's a job here if I want it.'

Jeremy James was pleased that she felt better, and it seemed to him that working in a hotel could be a lot of fun. You could talk to people on the telephone, for one thing. And for another, you could make sure that everybody had eggs and bacon for their breakfast. If he'd been Mrs Robinson, he'd have taken the job straight away. But even though Mrs Robinson was very small, she was grown-up, and grown-ups can be as strange as dinosaurs.

'We'd better tell the lady that Mrs Robinson doesn't want the job,' he said rather sadly.

'I think,' said Daddy, 'the lady already knows.'

When they got back to Welbeck Street, Mrs Robinson asked them to come to her office. There she went to a pile of books behind another pile of books beside a box of books under a table of books, and pulled out a book. It was a very big book.

'This, Jeremy James,' she said, 'is for you.'

She handed it over to him, and on the front cover was a picture that he recognized immediately.

'It's Dippy Dopus!' he cried. 'Look, Daddy, it's Dippy Dopus! Thank you very, very much, Mrs Robinson!'

He gave Mrs Robinson an even bigger kiss than he'd given to the policewoman, and when he'd kissed her, he noticed that she was smiling. Like the long-faced woman, she suddenly seemed brighter and sunnier.

Daddy and Jeremy James said goodbye to Mrs Robinson, and went out into the street. Jeremy James was holding his big book of dinosaurs under one arm, and his other hand was in Daddy's.

'London people are not happy,' said Jeremy James as they walked towards the car park, 'but they *could* be happy if they did a bit more smiling.'

CHAPTER FIFTEEN

Goodbye, London

Surprisingly, the car park had not moved from where it had been before, and the car had stayed in exactly the same space where they had left it. Daddy and Jeremy James found them both with no trouble at all.

'I'm learning,' said Daddy. 'The secret, Jeremy James, is to make mental notes of where things are. You don't just leave things and walk away. You say to yourself: "This is where it is", and then afterwards you remember. Simple. Now then, where's the parking ticket?'

Unfortunately, Daddy had forgotten to remember where the parking ticket was. He soon found where it was not. It was not in his coat or his jacket or his trousers. Nor was it in his bag. It wasn't in Jeremy James's bag either. And it wasn't on the front seat of the car, or the back seat, and it wasn't on the ledge under the windscreen, and it wasn't in the glove compartment.

'I must have lost it,' said Daddy.

Jeremy James thought Daddy must have lost it,

too, because otherwise, why were they looking for it? It was while Daddy was searching through his pockets for the fifth time that Jeremy James discovered where he had lost it. Jeremy James was sitting in the driver's seat, holding the steering wheel. As he couldn't see through the windscreen, he leaned over to look out of the open driver's door, and happened to notice that there was a pocket in the door. Sticking out of the pocket was a very tickety looking piece of paper.

'Is this it, Daddy?' asked Jeremy James.

'Of course!' said Daddy. 'I put it in there so that I wouldn't lose it!'

Daddy next applied his clever new method to finding the way out of London. He sat in the car and studied the map, memorizing directions and names of roads.

'I think I've got it,' he said at last. 'Concentration and memory, that's how to do it.'

He strapped Jeremy James into his seat, started the car, and away they went up the twisty tunnel as far as the exit barrier. There Daddy paid something called 'a small fortune', the barrier rose, and they drove the rest of the way up the street.

'Ah!' said Daddy. 'Now then, is it left, or is it right?'

Daddy's clever new method led to the same result as his old method, and soon they were driving through whatever streets of London happened to be in front of them. Jeremy James was no longer interested in the streets of London, though. He was busy watching his old friend Diplodocus munching a mouthful of grass from a riverbank, while on the other side of the page his old friend Tyrannosaurus was munching a mouthful of neck from a Deadosaurus.

At least, Jeremy James thought he was watching them. But twice he suddenly found his book of dinosaurs lying on the seat beside him. The first occasion was when he woke up just in time for some refreshments at the motorway service station. He was very good at waking up for refreshments. He was good at making them disappear, too. His old friends Diplodocus and Tyrannosaurus could not have munched the egg sandwich or the chocolate fudge cake any more efficiently than Jeremy James did.

On the second occasion, the car had stopped outside the house that he knew and loved better than any other house in the world. Mummy had already opened the front door, and gave him a hug and a kiss as he bounded in.

'Jem Jem home Londy!' cried Jennifer, leaping to her feet in the playpen and shaking the bars.

'Jem Jem Londy,' said Christopher, sitting beside her.

Going away was nice, but Jeremy James decided that coming home was even nicer. Then Mummy told him to go and have a wash, and he wondered if perhaps going away was nicer after all.

'Well, Jeremy James,' said Mummy, as they sat at

the table that evening, 'what did you like most in London?'

Jeremy James thought hard.

'The Dippy Dopus,' he said, 'and the bell tower, and Mrs Robinson.'

'And what did you like least?' asked Daddy.

'The Pry Monster,' said Jeremy James. 'And breakfast.'

He told Mummy all about the things he and Daddy had seen and done, and the people they'd met. She laughed about the pigeon lady and Number Coo, she gasped at the story of Polly Tishuns, she said 'Ts, ts!' about Timothy riding the dinosaur, she smiled at how Jeremy James had tried to get Mrs Robinson a job, and he didn't tell her about dialling nine-nine-nine.

'Of course,' said Daddy, 'there were loads of things we didn't see. We never went to the zoo, or the Tower of London, or St Paul's Cathedral, or Westminster Abbey.'

'You'd need to spend at least a week there to see *all* the sights,' said Mummy.

'Then we'd need to spend two weeks,' said Jeremy James.

'Why two weeks?' asked Mummy

'One week to see them,' said Jeremy James, 'and one week for Daddy to find them.'